Vicious

Chloe Spencer

SLASHIC HORROR
PRESS

ISBN-13: 978-0-9756380-8-8

Edited by David-Jack Fletcher

Interior Design by David-Jack Fletcher

Cover Design by Ruth Anna Evans

Other titles by Chloe Spencer

Adult Books
Vicarious
An Affinity for Formaldehyde
Mewing

YA Books
Monstersona
Haunting Melody

For every woman who thought she was unlovable for one reason or another, may you someday find the one who holds you close.

Content Warnings

Vicious contains graphic depictions of violence, gore, blood, death and mutilation of dead bodies, mentions of domestic violence, discussions of child sexual abuse, fatphobia, body-shaming, homophobia and use of homophobic slurs, vomit, drug use and brief depictions of addiction, and consensual BDSM and edge-play.

Please note: it's not safe to insert a tube of lipstick anywhere in your body.

One

A LONG TIME AGO, Gertie went for midnight drives with a person she loved. Now, twenty years and some change later, she was going for a midnight drive with a different lover. They were driving for the same reasons she had driven with her late husband, Jack, back then: to get away from polite society and enjoy each other's company.

But this time, to bury a dead body.

Shifting her grip on the steering wheel, Gertie glanced over at her girlfriend, Bea, who had her feet propped up on the dash, eyes closed in blissful slumber. This had been long overdue. The body of Earl, the fixer Gertie hired to clean up a few murders she orchestrated, was rotting in trash bags in the bed of her pickup. In late winter they had buried him, and now that it was summer, they had to dig him up again: all five chopped up body parts.

You can't leave a body in the same place for too long. It'd be a rookie mistake to make. They were asking for the kids—June and River—to find it once the summer heat sunk into the earth and wrestled the stench up from underneath the eight layers of dirt they'd piled on it. Realizing this, and wanting to take a vacation together anyway, the two shopped around for a lakefront vacation home with a good number of private acres. With the keys to their getaway, they had a perfect burial ground where no one would come knocking.

The tires of her pickup crunched along the bumpy dirt road, and the house loomed in the distance. It was a gorgeous A-frame cabin with tall, glossy windows, surrounded by several planter boxes full of flowers. Gertie had paid good money for landscapers to spruce it up before they arrived.

She wanted everything to be perfect for this weekend.

"Gertie."

"No, I'm not looking."

"One more time, come on."

Gertie looked up, mouth stretched in a thin line, trying not to laugh. Bea held Earl's decapitated head between her gloved hands like a soccer ball. The sockets of his eyes had hollowed out, the leathery skin now thin and worn in spots. When she shook it, clumps of unmentionable flesh and rot fell on the ground like confetti.

"Where's—your—head—a-a-a-at?"

"Hilarious."

"Wait, I got another one. Want me to give you some head?"

"You're a dork."

"You love me."

"I do. But honey, can you toss the man's skull in the hole before you get sick?"

Bea chuckled before turning around and throwing it into the hole. "Slam dunk!"

Exhausted, Gertie rubbed her eyes but smiled at her ridiculousness. She watched as Bea retrieved her shovel, then resumed her position beside the grave. Bea grunted as she thrust it deeper into the earth, tossing another mound of dirt over her shoulder. Mud smeared her cheeks like an unfashionable rouge. Gertie found it funny because Bea would never be caught dead in makeup.

Bea dumped the remaining body parts in the hole, then set aside the trash bags to burn later. Wiping off her hands, she set to work on filling it. Gertie sat in patient silence, answering emails from her phone and reviewing next week's school board agenda items. In the background, the truck's engine hummed, the radio playing music in an attempt to keep them alert and awake. Gertie half-wanted to curl up in the truck bed that still reeked of human rot and not wake up until tomorrow's moon hung in the night sky.

But she wasn't *that* selfish. At least, not anymore.

"You want some water?"

"Nah. If I drink water, it might ruin the sexiness of my muscles." Bea flexed to demonstrate, and Gertie giggled. "You know that's what Hugh Jackman had to do for his role as Wolverine in *Logan*, right? Worked out, then dehydrated himself."

"If I recall correctly, that wasn't a safe exercise method."

"So you're intimately familiar with the works of Hugh Jackman?"

"Intimately familiar with the time he made the cover of *Good Housekeeping,* you mean?"

"Have you not seen the movie, babe?"

"No, I haven't, but if I promise to watch it, will you drink some water?" Gertie cracked open the cooler and passed her a water bottle.

Bea wiped her hands on her jeans and accepted it, pouring it over her head a little before swallowing a few gulps. Gertie pulled at the collar of her sweatshirt, watching as some of the water soaked through Bea's ribbed-knit tank top, revealing the glistening ivory skin beneath.

What a sight.

Satisfied, Bea finished filling in the hole, packing the dirt with her shovel. Gertie sprinkled grass seed and water over the top of it. Within a few weeks, this patch of earth would blend in with the surrounding forest. Earl would become mulch. Seemed like a poetic end for a fixer who was also a gardener. He'd probably appreciate it.

Gertie retrieved a wet wipe from her purse and wiped away the sweat and dirt on Bea's face. Bea's eyelids fluttered closed, satisfied.

"That feels *so* good."

A new song shifted onto the radio, and Bea's eyes snapped open, wide with excitement.

"I haven't heard this one in ages." She grabbed Gertie's hand, pulling her to her feet.

"Ohh Bea, we're both so sweaty and gross."

"I can think of other times we were sweaty and gross, and you didn't mind it one bit."

"*Beatrice.*" Gertie's lips twisted into a smirk, and she assumed the position as the lead.

Pressed chest to chest, she could feel Bea's heart quivering with excitement. The melody of "Tiny Dancer" echoed from the speakers, drowning out the sounds of the surrounding night. Bea laughed as Gertie spun her around. The reek of decaying flesh and mud was so thick in the air they could almost taste it on their tongues, but they didn't care. As long as their hands were on each other's bodies, they were having a good time.

"Thank you for doing this. I know burying a body isn't exactly the best start to a romantic weekend. And I'd hoped we'd get here earlier to check out that nice supper club, but that stupid meeting ran late, and—"

"Gertie, relax! We can go tomorrow. Besides, I didn't know this weekend was *supposed* to be romantic."

"Y-yeah, well, uh... No kids. And in our brand new lake house." Gertie twirled her before pulling her back in. "I'd love to make the most of our time alone."

"We are." Bea pressed her cheek against hers. "And y'know, this is morbid, but—also kinda hot, right? That we share this dark secret together?"

"Your ability to look on the bright side of things is fascinating, angel."

Chuckling, Bea leaned in, resting her chin on Gertie's shoulder. Suddenly she felt heavier in this moment; a telltale sign she was more tired than she claimed to be.

Gertie smiled as she kissed her cheek. "Let's get you to bed."

Bea cracked an eye open. "To sleep, or to—"

"*Bea-trice!* It's three in the morning. Where do you find the energy?"

"One thing about me, baby, I can always find the energy."

Gertie laughed. Bea chuckled, crouching down to pick up the shovel. As she turned back to the truck, though, she noticed something odd.

Her girlfriend was down on one knee.

"Gertie."

Her voice was unrecognizable as it left her mouth, strangled by tears that hadn't yet sprung to her eyes. She staggered backward, jaw slack. Gertie reached into her pocket and withdrew a small black box. With trembling hands, she cracked it open, revealing the silver band within it. No glittering diamond, no sparkly superficial things.

Only the promise of a beautiful future.

"I wanted to do this at that restaurant, because—I mean, you should see the pictures online, it's gorgeous—but I can't wait any longer to start the rest of our lives. So... Beatrice Rosemary Robinson."

"*Stop.*" Bea cackled in disbelief, hands flinging upwards to cover her mouth and nose. Tears welled in her quivering eyes. "*Gertrude.*"

"When we met in that Chinese restaurant again, I had no idea how hard I would fall for you. Since you've wandered back into my life, what was once shrouded in darkness, you've now filled with the light of your smile. You are the rhythm in my song, the morning star to my dark night, the peanut butter to my banana."

Bea laughed. "Is that a dick joke in your proposal?"

"Might be." Gertie winked, but in the next moment, her confidence evaporated. The earnestness in her brown eyes grew, and her voice trembled as she spoke. "These past eight months have been nothing short of blissful, and a lifetime with you—well, I'm a rich woman, but that would bring me happiness no money could buy. So Bea, will you marry me?"

"Oh my god—*Gertie.* Yes, yes, oh my god, yes. That's all I've ever wanted."

Gertie slipped the ring onto her finger. Squealing with delight, Bea embraced her, her kiss forceful and fiery. Gertie laughed against her lips.

Never had a funeral been such a joyful occasion.

Two

"I CAN'T BELIEVE IT." Bea examined her ring in awe. "I had no idea you were planning this."

They were in bed now, and although dawn would break in a few hours, the two had done everything but sleep. Their coveted steak knife, which Bea loved to have held against her throat—rested on the nightstand, and the sheets were soaked in more ways than one. Bea buried herself against the pillows, and Gertie straddled her back. Red handprints marred the surface of Bea's muscular ass, and she couldn't help but smile at the sight.

She planted kisses against her neck before squirting lotion onto her hands and lathering it into Bea's shoulders, working deep into the muscle tissue. "Really? You didn't suspect it?"

"When would I have—*oof*, ow, babe, please be gentle."

"Sorry!" Another kiss. "Remember a while back, when I asked you for your thoughts on weddings?"

"Oh. But I thought you were talking about the ones we had in the past."

Every year, Gertie celebrated her wedding anniversary with Jack by breaking out the photo albums and blasting songs from their reception playlist through the house. In the past she used the day as an opportunity to tell June stories about her dad, but at this point, she'd heard them all. This year, Bea joined her in looking through them.

While Gertie and Jack married no more than three days after high school, Bea, in contrast, did not marry for love. She had lived a tortured existence, trying her absolute hardest to stay in the closet. She only ended up with Westley, her ex-husband, because she was looking to escape her parents. With no post-secondary education and no job prospects, and in her early 20s, she followed him to Kentucky, planning to ditch him and head to Memphis. The night before she was supposed to leave, she discovered she was pregnant with Trevor, and when Westley found out about her pregnancy, he forced her to stay with him. Their wedding had no happy photos, no cake to cut, and Bea had to wear an ugly white dress that somewhat hid her baby bump.

Whenever Gertie heard the stories about Westley, she'd think the death she'd dealt onto him—cracking open his head with a meat cleaver—had been far too easy.

One night, while poring through the photos, Gertie asked about her feelings on marriage, and Bea had told her, "It would be nice to marry someone for the right reasons this time, instead of the wrong ones."

Gertie was hellbent on being all the right reasons.

Bea laughed. "I guess I thought it was too soon."

"Would we be us if we didn't move a hundred miles per hour?"

"I don't think so." Giggling, Bea rolled onto her back, and Gertie snuggled up beside her. "I swore when I divorced Westley I'd only remarry if I found someone who was worth it."

"I'm glad you think so."

"How could I not? You spoil me rotten." Bea kissed her cheek. "If anything, it's me who's not worthy of you. Like, how'd a loser like me bag a woman this hot?"

"Don't say that. You've made my dreams come true, angel." It was true. She had. When Bea had entered her life, gone was the loneliness, the heartache, the suffering through the mundane day-to-day. "And because of that, I'm going to make sure you have the wedding of your dreams."

"The wedding of *our* dreams."

"Well, that goes without saying. But *yours*. You never got the fairytale dream that I got."

Bea's voice ran thin. "That's because I didn't think fairytales happened for people like me."

"We have time to plan."

"Yeah. Um... I may not have ideas for that yet, but..." Bea's voice thinned, and she swallowed, as though parched. "I... I want to change my name to yours."

"To Taylor?"

"No. To Burns. I don't think you should change your name back to your maiden one. It wouldn't be right. You—you loved Jack, and you should honor that. You should have a name that matches your daughter's. But I don't want to be associated with my family. I-If you'll let me, I want his name, too."

"Hmm. I kinda like the sound of Beatrice Burns."

Bea giggled. "Me too."

"I don't think my in-laws would mind that." Jack's parents had long moved away from their state, having retired in Savannah, Georgia. When they learned about Bea, they were ecstatic for her. Sometimes she wished they were still around. Then again, if they lived close by, they'd likely find out about her diabolical acts. And she couldn't stand to break their hearts. They were good people, through and through, as Jack had been.

Gertie closed her eyes, ready to let sleep take her. Bea squeezed her body tight and kissed her cheek.

"Night, honey. Thanks for making me the happiest woman in the world."

What Bea didn't know is that they were both competing for that title at this moment.

Three

AFTER A WEEKEND SPENT frolicking on a pontoon, sipping margaritas and having too much sex, the soon-to-be-weds returned home to find other cars piled in their driveway and heart-shaped balloons anchored to the flowerbeds. Familiar faces hauled in so many bottles of champagne it was like they were stocking a speakeasy.

Gertie's heart hit her stomach as she climbed out of the car. "She didn't."

She unloaded the luggage as Bea greeted some of the guests, grinning ear to ear. As Gertie heard them murmur their congratulations, anger tickled the back of her neck.

June had thrown them a surprise engagement party.

Gertie had told her daughter what this weekend was meant for, in part to be a good mother and let her know about major life changes, but also to dissuade her from peeking around in the truck while they packed in a dead body. June, sweetheart that she was, was overjoyed to learn they were getting married.

"Love you both," she said, "but the admissions offices are going to *eat up* the fact I have two moms and a dead dad."

And that had been the first time Gertie truly realized June was her daughter. She had never been prouder. But this? *This* was a bit of a problem. Not only were they tired, but Gertie had been hoping to keep their engagement under wraps. Planning a wedding was stressful no matter if it was your first or fifth, and she didn't need any political opponents to know she would be potentially distracted from her duties—not when she was setting her sights on a state senate position within the next year or two. While Gertie was only half a year into her school board position—of which she was expected to serve four years—it was never too early to consider her next career moves.

The women shuffled into the house and were immediately greeted with a toast and several congratulations. They accepted this with nervous smiles and sweaty faces. Bea managed to break away from the crowd to haul their stuff up to their room. Throngs of people gathered in the living room and in the kitchen. An open punch bowl rested on the dining room table along with an array of refreshments: cupcakes, finger sandwiches, and one of those god-awful veggie platters with the carrots that tasted like chalk. A Costco sheet cake sat in the center, reading, "Congrats on Your Engagement!"

Goddamn it, June, did you put all of this on your credit card?

"Mommy!"

Gertie turned to see her daughter in a bright pink teacup dress and matching strappy sandals. Her gorgeous blond curls were piled on top of her head in a messy bun, making her look like a Barbie doll fresh out of the box. In one hand she held a red Solo cup full of punch, which Gertie desperately hoped wasn't spiked with liquor, but knowing her opportunistic daughter, it probably was.

"Congratulations!" June squealed as she one-arm hugged her mother, oblivious to her stiffness. The liquid sloshed around in her cup, a few droplets spilling over the edge. "What do you think about the party?"

"It's lovely..." Gertie muttered, eyes flickering around the room. No one was in the backyard—good. They wouldn't notice the fresh patch of grass beside the daisies. "But honey, we—"

"Gertie!" A familiar, crowing voice echoed out. Gertie turned to see Kellyanne, the woman who had succeeded her in the Trinity Oaks PTA. Her eyes were blotchy red, lower lip trembling. *Christ alive.* "There's the woman who made me believe in love again!"

"Kellyanne!" *You're literally married, what are you fucking talking about?* Gertie smiled through clenched teeth, accepting her embrace. "It's been a while!"

"You've been busy making moves on that school board, girlie!" Kellyanne dabbed at her eyes with the sleeves of her mumu. "Oh dear, I can't tell you how happy I am for you. I remember telling Mis—well, you-know-who—at the first dance you brought her to, I said, *This has to be the one. She's gotta be it.* The two of you couldn't keep your hands off each other."

Gertie stumbled the rest of her way through that conversation before being assaulted by another barrage of well-wishes from other partygoers. There was no way in hell she was going to make it out of this situation, so she was going to have to go along with it.

It wasn't until she felt Bea's hand at the small of her back again that her seizing heart relaxed.

"Hey babe," she said to her, and then to the guests, "Sorry about that! You know this one, she packs a lot. Always overprepared."

Gertie smirked as she pressed herself into Bea's side, wrapping her arm around her waist. Glued together, they made their way through the rest of the party and schmoozed. Bea was always the social butterfly; she had been since they were kids. She remembered the most minuscule details about people's lives when Gertie couldn't even remember their names. Bea was her lover, but also a valuable asset to her career, and it was obvious from how her eyes twinkled and her skin glowed that she was proud of it.

"Mom, Bea," June said. She smiled and motioned for them to follow her. "You haven't seen the best part yet."

In one corner of the front hall, June had assembled a table. Memories from the past year were scattered across its surface, along with a few more curious inclusions. Gertie and Bea stared in shock. Photos of them in their classes, each adorned with a red-lettered year and date. One of them was from the third grade, the year Bea had moved to Appledale. Gertie hovered at the back of the classroom, brown eyes stretched wide with fear. Bea beamed from ear to ear as she stood beside her other friends. In the furthest reaches of her mind, Gertie remembered this day. Bea had harassed her that morning, telling her she was going to give her a "surprise she would never forget." That surprise ended up being shredded rolls of toilet paper in each of the bathroom stalls, leaving her without a way to wipe her ass.

But June had no idea their relationship had a foul and hateful beginning. She was oblivious to it, rosy cheeked and cheerful, waiting for their responses.

Gertie's fingers brushed over a photo of Bea in middle school, shortly before the infamous tampon-eating incident, and before Bea's paternal uncle had been arrested. The light in Bea's eyes had died by the time she reached this age, fully cognizant of the hell she was subjected to. No smile remained on her face.

Gertie squeezed Bea's hand and offered June a kind smile. "Thank you, honey."

At that moment, June skipped away to attend something else. Bea stared at the photo like it was taken from a crime scene. When she spoke, she sounded like a ghost, and her face was so devoid of color, she might as well have been one.

"My hair was so long back then."

"It was." Gertie's fingers combed through her choppy blond waves, traced the shaved edges behind her ears. "I much prefer the look you have now."

"Thanks."

Gertie kissed her cheek, and Bea's expression softened. For a few minutes, they stared at their past-selves, at two little girls who had hated each other viciously, but would grow up to fall in love after a lifetime of adversity. For Gertie, it was surreal. This woman had once been her worst nightmare—a nightmare she had wanted to end by her own two hands—and now almost every night, she'd give her the stuff of sweetest dreams.

If said "sweet dreams" involved holding a knife to someone's throat while you absolutely obliterated their pussy.

"Should we—should we tell her?"

"What good would that do? Our kids don't need to know every nefarious thing we've done." Gertie's voice dropped several octaves. "God *knows* what they hear at night…"

"Hey!" Bea giggled. "I told you to buy that gag."

"But then I don't get to hear your lovely voice scream out my name. Plus I have an irrational fear of the ball breaking off the gag and choking you."

"Wouldn't be the end of the world. I could die having an incredible orgasm."

"Hard pass. We need a little less death in our lives. From here on out, the only kind of blood I want to shed is my uterine lining. At least until menopause kicks in."

"You know something? I was almost perimenopausal before I moved in here with you."

"When our cycles started syncing, I was worried we'd have even more bodies to bury."

"!" Bea giggled again. Her head swiveled around, as if to check to see who overheard them. "Huh. Where's River?"

Wait. That's right. Where was their fair-haired son? The two sifted through the party, attempting to find him. He was standing in the kitchen beside his boyfriend, Holland, who he had met on the soccer team after transferring to Trinity Oaks. They started "dating" within the past couple of months, and for eighth graders, that meant holding hands, playing video games, and sharing the same soda can. Holland had a head of curly hair and ochre-brown skin, and a charming smile, one that nearly blinded Gertie as she walked into the room. She had to rub her eyes to readjust. He was almost the polar opposite of morose and subdued River, but then again, opposites attracted—the same for her and Bea.

River looked up from where he was organizing cupcakes on a multi-tiered stand. "Congratulations Mom and Other-Mom!"

"Thanks, Riv!" Bea tousled his hair and kissed his forehead. "Why aren't you enjoying the party?"

"I gotta put out more cupcakes."

"Ooh," Gertie said. "Did you make the lemon ones with the vanilla bean frosting?"

"Oh, Gertie." He gave her a wry smirk. "I made that, *and* the maple bacon chocolates."

The women helped themselves to cupcakes and champagne, then watched as the boys exited the room with the stand, ready to restock a catering table.

Gertie licked the frosting from her fingers. "How much do you want to bet that Holland stayed the night this weekend?"

"Christ," Bea groaned. "You don't think they did anything, did you?"

"I mean, if *I* had been left alone in a house with my boyfriend as a teenager?"

"*Gertrude.*"

"Opportunity of a lifetime, all I'm saying. I'd much rather have lost my virginity in a bed than the backseat of a truck. Jack had to hang one of my feet from the seatbelt like it was a stirrup."

"That's not funny, Gertie! I *knew* I should've had the talk with him but I just didn't—I mean, fourteen is so young!"

"Yeah, but looking back, I think that's about when Jack and I were getting into those sorts of things. By fifteen for sure."

"Ugh... Do you think he has condoms in his room?"

"I don't know. You can always snoop in there later. Not like he's hiding anything in places we wouldn't have been clever enough to try when we were kids."

She knew River couldn't have been hiding anything in Trevor's room. Gertie had set up a camera there in case anyone tried to snoop, but also told the kids it was there "in case Trevor ever came back." Little shit always found ways to shimmy down the trellis or the drain pipe, even when he had been grounded.

Goddamn, just thinking about how horrible he was gave her heart palpitations.

Gertie washed her hands in the sink. "If June let that happen, though, she's getting grounded."

"Aww, Gertie. Don't do that. She tried so hard to make this special for us. If she does know, she was probably trying to do her little brother a solid." Bea smiled as she sipped from her flute. "Besides, I thought you were more sex positive than that."

"Teenagers have better things to do. Algebra to learn."

"Some kids want to learn biology instead. You were one of those kids once!"

Gertie blushed. "Touché."

"I would've *killed* to date a girl in high school. The only thing I ever did was offer to teach other girls how to kiss at slumber parties."

"And people took you up on that?"

"I had a new student every other weekend."

"Wow. The closet was made of glass."

"Sparkly pretty pink glass so none of the girls thought otherwise. By the time my senior year came around and I never had a boyfriend, they finally put it together. Once cheer season was over, so was my social life."

"Aww." Gertie nudged her. "At least your hard work paid off. You're an expert kisser."

Bea pressed her lips to her ear, chuckling. Delicious goosebumps tickled Gertie's arms as she heard her whisper, "I can tell."

Four

B Y FOUR O'CLOCK, MOST of the guests had trickled out, in search of more food. June began to wash the dishes while River attended to the trash.

"What're we doing for dinner tonight?" River asked, glancing at the disastrous state of the kitchen.

Ugh. Times like this, Gertie wished she had a maid, but she was too paranoid to let strangers wander around the house unattended. Besides, it taught the kids basic life skills and kept them from being spoiled little shits. An old PTA acquaintance of hers once said her son had no idea how to clean a toilet, and Gertie was horrified that a parent would let their child grow up to be so useless.

"Pizza?" she suggested, and the kids cheered. She smiled as she glanced in the direction of the backyard. Then her heart hit her stomach.

There was someone out there.

"Who is that?" Gertie whispered, nudging Bea with her elbow.

It was a man—not tall, but broad-shouldered, and for some reason he was wearing a cowboy hat and a tight white polo that clung to his muscular frame. He even had cowboy boots on, for Chrissakes. Dude looked like he had gotten lost on the way to the rodeo.

"Uh..." Gertie looked at June. "You want to call in the order? I'm going to say goodbye to our guest."

June gave her a soapy thumbs up and returned to her task. Gertie motioned for Bea to follow her and the two exited into the backyard. The man walked up and down the rows of flowers and crops, nodding like he was appreciating the craftsmanship.

"Hey there," Bea said, a cheery smile plastered on her face. "Thanks for coming out. You'll get a wedding invite once we've set the date!"

The man lifted his head, and tilted back his hat, as if the brim was so wide, he couldn't see them from underneath it. His face was interesting. A nose with the nostrils turned upwards, scraggly mustache hairs on his upper lip and cheeks, and overstated sideburns. Definitely recognizable, and yet, Gertie recognized no part of him.

"I just got here," he said, his voice gruff. It felt forced, guttural; like it wasn't the way he truly spoke. He crouched down to one of the rows and tapped the sign for the tomatoes. "What kind are these?"

"Beefsteak," Gertie said.

"That color is gorgeous. What kind of fertilizer do you use?"

"Uh..." Gertie crossed her arms. "I don't buy fertilizer, I use what's in my compost pile." She pointed to the back corner of the yard, where a chicken wire bin sat, holding the decaying contents. "And that's from mowing the yard, dead plants, and food waste."

"Ahh. Stuff's a little too green, from what I see. You know you gotta make the brown equal the green. Fifty-fifty. Add your empty egg cartons to it and I think you'll get rid of some of that smell. The carbon'll aerate the stuff." He shrugged his shoulders. "Though what do I know? You're clearly managing fine on your own."

"I'm sorry," Gertie said, "have we met?"

"No," he said. "But you might know who I used to work for."

Fuck. Gertie's arm swung out in defense of Bea, as if to shield her from him. He looked between the two, a wry smirk on his face. She couldn't believe she hadn't noticed the embroidered logo on his shirt until now.

Rose Landscaping Services.

This man used to work for Earl.

He stood up, and looked past the women, at the house. Gertie glanced back, and saw June was in the kitchen window, still washing some of the platters from the party.

"Nah," he said, keeping an eye on her. "I'm not here for anything foul. Wouldn't do that to you in front of your kids."

"Then what are you here for?" Bea snapped.

"I know what happened. He told me about it before he went over to your house." The man reached up to pluck the hat from his head, and he held it over his heart. *What the fuck? Who is he, John Wayne?* "I come here on humble, happy terms."

"Trust us," Bea said, "we don't want to be associated with the likes of your employer anymore."

"I am my own employer now. I'm the de facto owner of the company should Daddy have ever become incapacitated. And I'm guessing he's more than incapacitated, right?" He gestured to the suspicious patch of grass covering the hole that used to house his body. "May I ask where you've buried him?"

"We don't know what you're talking about," Gertie said, choosing her words carefully.

"You've got 'guilty' written all over your face, ma'am. Look, you can trust me. I'm not wearing a wire or anything. Pat me down if you'd like." He spread his arms wide as a scarecrow, and slowly twirled around. With the thinness of his shirt, it looked like he was right; there was no wire to be hid. No earpieces, either. He tugged his pockets inside out as well, for good measure. "Can we talk now?"

"There's nothing to talk about," Gertie replied.

"Look, I understand the hostility, but the kind of conversation I want to have is one that can't happen over the phone. Just my luck I happened to come at an inopportune time. Which, congratulations on your engagement by the way."

He looked between the two of them with an affectionate smile that made Gertie's stomach bubble with nausea. Panic pulsed within her chest. *Shit fuck shit.* What was she supposed to do? The kids were in the house. Even if she managed to get a weapon to kill the guy in time, there was no way they wouldn't see her. And no way she could keep Bea out of the crossfire. She had to hear him out.

"Who are you?" she asked.

"Name's Kayle."

"What—Kayle? Like the vegetable?"

He nodded.

"And what business would you have with us, Kayle? Another shakedown? Because I've got no patience for something like that."

"Of course not. You're a busy woman. School board member, chair of the winter toy drive, and now, a bride-to-be. And rumor has it you're eyeing a spot on the state senate, if I'm correct?"

She didn't reply. Bea's hand clenched her arm, her fingers digging into her flesh. She could feel the bruises expanding across the canvas of her skin, but didn't dare look down to see them.

"See, I voted for you," he said. "Even after what you did, I voted for you. You ran a good campaign, and you get the job done. You've already gotten more funding for afterschool programs, and you've fought back against a few book bans. I find that mighty admirable for someone who's only been in office a few months."

"Um, thank you for your support?"

He grinned. "Much obliged. Now…" He kicked at a little mound of dirt, and reached over to pluck a tomato from the vine. "The way I see it, you're more of a vigilante than a serial killer. Seeing how you only kill people who have wronged you or someone you loved in some way."

Gertie considered this. Back when she waged her act of revenge against Bea, she had killed her parents in order to upend her whole life—and also, because they were abusive fuckwads. She killed Westley when he came looking for Bea, after he had stalked River's Instagram to find her. And Trevor—that violent bastard of a boy—attempted to sexually assault June, and he was not going to put his hands on her and live to tell the tale. All of them, in their own way, had wronged Gertie, and posed significant dangers to society. Well, Bea's parents didn't, but they had turned a blind eye to the abuse she had experienced at the hands of her uncle, so they got what was coming to them.

Ehh, fuck it. She'd take vigilante over a murderer any day.

A teasing smile spread across Kayle's lips. "See, I figured you'd agree with me. But Daddy and I didn't always see eye to eye."

"You keep calling him that. Was he your father?" Odd. A hitman was a private person, but surely he would have said something about being a parent, considering she was one herself. That was the kind of factoid even the tightest lipped people would slip.

Kayle shook his head, lips pressed in a near-invisible line. He placed his hat on his head again, then reached into his pocket and withdrew a few crumpled papers and a tiny vial full of soot. It took her a second to realize it was tobacco. He laid a paper flat in his palm and tapped some of the tobacco onto it.

"Daddy's what I called him."

"O-oh. He was—he was—"

"Queer, yes."

"Wow." Gertie said. She looked between him and Bea. "Now I feel kinda bad."

Bea stared at her. "What? Why?"

"Because it feels like killing one of our own. Is there a gay code we're expected to follow? Did we violate it?"

Kayle shook his head. "Ain't no code but a code of honor, ma'am. Far's I'm concerned, you followed it fine. He set foot on your property and tried to strongarm you into a deal not even the most hopeless of fools would make. He wasn't all that good at negotiating. And not too bright either. You remember that car wreck? Where you left all those footprints?"

"What? No. I didn't..."

"Course you don't remember leaving those footprints. No one did, because I cleaned them up for you. Aww, don't look at me all concerned now. For as much as we were lovers we were also business partners. And like I said, we didn't always agree." He wet his lips and used it to roll his cigarette. "Now me, I wouldn't have demanded a cut of your fortune outright, but I'd love to have a little piece of the pie."

Here we fucking go again. Gertie resisted the urge to groan and swallowed the lump of anger rising in the back of your throat. "What are you suggesting?"

"Five thousand a month to attend to your 'gardens'. Extra five to ten thou per person you'd need buried in them. Think of the first five thou like a monthly membership fee. A Netflix subscription. You keep me on call in case you need dirt on anyone, strong-arm someone, all of that good shit. You kill? You pay more. And you pay the monthly fee so you make sure I—"

"Keep quiet?" Gertie asked.

Kayle nodded. "You got it."

"Kayle, while I'm ecstatic you're not threatening me for 50 million dollars, I have to say, I... I don't think I'm going to have—"

"We agreed we'd keep things clean from now on," Bea said, squeezing Gertie's shoulder. "So your services won't be needed."

"But my services as a dirt-digger?" His smile moved to accommodate the cigarette, which he lit up. "You can't be telling me this one ain't never going to need a P.I. again. She'd been using one for years, ma'am. Long before she met you."

"Well, I could use your expertise..." If he had Earl's knowledge and capabilities, he would be more useful to her as an ally than an enemy, anyways. Gertie couldn't take on more enemies, especially if she wanted to avoid bloodshed and building a graveyard on the property of her 1.3 million dollar lake home. "But why would I pay you on a monthly basis? Why not pay you on a task-by-task basis? Wouldn't that make you more money in the long run?"

"No," he said, chuckling. "If you paid me on a task-by-task basis, and you manage to play nice with all your little government friends, that means I don't get anything. You paying me monthly means I at least get something. Think of it this way. I'm on call 24/7. Your own personal P.I. and hitman. I'd have no other clients, unlike the others you've worked with in the past."

As strange as this was, it was a good deal. Gertie knew herself well: she played dirty, and that meant she needed to dig up dirt. The P.I. she had used in the past, [REDACTED], had exited the picture when she had asked for a referral to Earl's business, not wanting to be associated with potential murders. This meant that for the past few months, Gertie had been responsible for doing her own investigatory work, which was exhausting and time-consuming. Scouring websites and social media websites were *not* her area of expertise—for Christ's sake, she barely knew how to use Instagram.

Gertie squinted at him. "I'm not sure what your game is…"

Bea elbowed her. "It sounds like a good deal."

"There has to be a catch."

"No catch. The next time you want to take down a predator, I want in." He dragged on the cigarette and blew a perfect cloud of smoke in the air, then adjusted his hat. "You don't have to give me your answer today, but—"

"Bad things will happen if I don't agree to this now, so…fine." Gertie sighed.

"You won't regret this, ma'am. I'll earn my keep."

"And if you don't, I'm still stuck with you," she grumbled.

He grinned. "Unfortunately." He tipped his hat. "See you 'round, ladies."

"Wait, do you have an autopay option? Because I'm a little too busy to cut a paper check every month."

Five

D AYS LIKE TODAY MADE Gertie wish she wasn't in politics. She woke up at 5 a.m., an ungodly time she never woke up at when she was on the PTA, and delivered a single kiss to Bea's sleeping head before showering and getting dressed. After loading a to-go cup with coffee and three sugars, she was off to work.

Before she started this position, Gertie envisioned working in a regal building akin to the state Capitol's, and instead, found herself spending long hours in a warehouse-like building adjacent to City Hall. She had tried to spruce up her dank little office with bright pops of color and items from Target's clearance section to no avail. At the very least, the sunlight was decent, although the place stunk of mildew. She'd go to the office, spend time reviewing emails, and then attend meetings throughout the day. The main school board met twice monthly, usually for hours into the night. She was also on additional committees—Budget and Fundraising, Safety and Wellness, and the ad hoc she created, Enrichment and Opportunity—that would have meetings on other days and evenings. Sometimes her calendar was empty, other days it was crammed back to back.

The worst part about being in charge of a school board was that these people were ill-equipped to make financial decisions. It was the same bullshit she dealt with being the PTA president at Trinity Oaks, only now instead of being responsible for managing maybe a couple tens of thousands of dollars every year (if the fundraisers went well), she was now responsible for millions.

And these people *loved* to piss their money away. Richard Branson, the big-dicked colleague who vetoed her suggestions for fun, owned an athletic shoe store and had filed for bankruptcy twice in the past. That bastard was friends with the superintendent, and in previous years, had voted to give him a raise. She suspected foul money was at play—it almost always was—but maybe now she'd leave that to Kayle to look into.

In between meetings, she would either eat a lunch Bea had packed, or meet somewhere for lunch. Since Bea had quit her job as a grocery clerk and taken over the household management duties, the homemade lunches were more frequent, much to Gertie's delight. Today, Bea had made a turkey sandwich topped with a roasted kale salad and chipotle aioli—her greatest talent was making kale taste halfway decent. Also, that thing she could do with her tongue.

Gertie nibbled on her sandwich while answering more emails and fantasizing about stabbing Richard in his smug fucking face. Last week he'd laughed at a couple of suggestions she made to a few budget line items, and the way the other men had chuckled reinforced how much of a boys' club this all was. With the PTA, she had to deal with cattiness, which was exhausting, but not as obnoxious as these misogynistic twats were.

And worse, she would be spending *more* time with some of these men tonight for the local woman's shelter charity gala. Not because they supported the cause, oh no, they wouldn't be so bold as to outright support women. They couldn't even be bothered to give a shit about the safety of the children. One of these fuckers—Arthur Cunningham—believed teachers should carry guns in schools, instead of investing in other safety measures. They were sure to tell Gertie they were going out of support for their "wives", which only sickened her more.

Her sole reprieve from the bullshit were her female colleagues, Winnie Tshele and Laura Gestafson. They were college educated, ambitious women who had worked hard to balance their careers while raising their children. These women didn't drink rosé for breakfast and fuss over what decorations needed to be color-matched like her PTA cohorts did, no, they dreamed big. They joined her ad hoc committee and were fighting with her to make it a standing one.

She would feel threatened by them if she didn't admire them so damn much. Besides, Gertie knew the bigger she aimed, the more friends she needed. And she couldn't lose focus by playing petty games of revenge or hiring P.I.s to unveil her friends' dirty secrets as she had done before—at least, not as often as before. She was aiming bigger now, bigger than she ever had: the school board wasn't her entire life as the PTA presidency had once been. No, it was a stepping stone to the state senate.

And for these like-minded women, if one of them won, they *all* won.

Finishing her sandwich, Gertie reached into her lunch box for the thing she loved most: the note. Bea would draw her little cartoons on Post-It notes. Today was a doodle of the two of them, with Bea giving her a kiss on the cheek... and squeezing her ass. *You're the apple of my eye.* Gertie chuckled. Bea had packed an apple along with the sandwich. *Adorable.*

"Gertie."

Gertie looked up from her desk, eyes bleary. Laura leaned against her doorway, her long white hair draping over her shoulders, straight as a shower curtain.

"If you're going to work hard today," she said, "you better play hard tonight at the gala."

When Bea saw what she was planning on wearing tonight, there was no way she wouldn't.

Gertie sprayed a little mousse into her hands and lathered it into her damp curls. She hated blow drying her hair—always gave her frizz—so she hoped her hair would dry on the way over. She stood in front of the bathroom mirror, crimping and scrunching to build its volume, wearing only her bra and underwear. Bea waltzed in from the closet door, fully dressed and ready to go. Her hair was slicked down against her head, giving her hair a Gatsby-esque appearance.

"Ahh, the perks of being butch," Gertie murmured, admiring the crispness of Bea's outfit. A blue plaid blazer with matching pants; a white shirt that had been tastefully unbuttoned to show enough of her clavicle and neck, which she felt an impulse to bite. "You look beautiful, angel."

Bea smiled and slid a hand around her waist, rubbing small circles on her soft, stretchmark-covered stomach. Her eyes traced the curves of her body with admiration, like a sculptor planning their next move. Gertie shivered, trying to resist her desires.

"Okay!" She tapped her fingers against Bea's wandering hand, motioning for her to leave her be.

"Is it time for tonight's fashion show? You gonna wear that little red number?"

"Actually..." She stepped into her high heels, examining them in the mirror again. They were black, about four inches tall, and had ribbons that twisted up and united at a bow at the top of her ankles. "Can you bring that black zip bag?"

Bea retrieved it from the closet.

Gertie blew on her freshly painted red nails, examining them. "Open it."

Confused, Bea pulled on the zipper, unveiling the midnight floor-length gown inside. It was studded with sequins and twinkled like a disco ball underneath their bathroom lights. As Bea pulled it out from the bag by its hanger, her eyes widened with excitement.

"Is this *strapless*?" she cried out.

For months, and for some reason unbeknownst to her, Bea had begged her to get a strapless dress, insisting she would, quote, "Look so hot, you'd burn the whole fucking place down." Most of Gertie's clothes hid her arms, which she was self-conscious of. She didn't mind wearing things that emphasized her tits and ass, but wearing a strapless dress felt like exposing too much of herself. She had fretted about slipping out of it, but Bea had been so insistent she tried it, saying, *What's the worst that could happen?*

Apparently Bea didn't consider a nip slip as one of those things. Actually, knowing her, it'd be a benefit.

"Yes, yes. Can you help me get it over my hips and zip up the dress?"

"Don't mind if I do," Bea replied, her voice breathless.

Supple rolls of fat cascaded down Gertie's back, the lip of her Spanx cresting over one. Bea's silver eyes fixated on it, as though mesmerized by its perfection. Smooth, peachy skin, with not a single blemish or scar. Constellations of freckles across the back of her shoulders and a variety of sunspots, no doubt earned from the hours she spent in the garden, painted its surface.

She was a work of art.

"How're you doing back there, champ?" Gertie asked, smirking.

Bea zipped up her dress. It was a perfect fit, hugging the curves of her hourglass body. Gertie's stomach somersaulted with desire. *Those eyes.* Bea's expression was oddly possessive, separate from the wanton, how-can-I-please-you-my-goddess eyes she was used to. Bea's lips brushed against her shoulder as her hands wound around her waist, fingers grazing suspiciously low. Although Gertie knew better—*god, she should know better*—she couldn't help but lean into Bea's touch.

"Gertie Burns, you've got no business being this sexy." Bea's fingers kneaded into her flesh. "Makes me want to keep you all to myself."

Gertie's eyelids fluttered as kisses pressed against her neck. "We're going to be late."

"I know." Bea's fingers gathered her shimmery skirt, tugging down her Spanx and underwear. She gasped. Goosebumps rippled across her now chilled thighs, but that space between them was unseasonably warm. "So tell me you want me to stop."

"You bitch."

Bea chuckled. Her Spanx was halfway down her thighs but her underwear still clung to her hips. Impatient, Bea's fingers dove beneath the lace, and Gertie's mouth parted in a pleasurable "O" of ecstasy. At the same time, a tremor of confusion coursed through her. This wasn't Bea's M.O. In the bedroom, the furthest she had ever "topped", so to speak, was when she was going down on her, and even then, Bea was still submissive, all sweet smiles and eyes so warm they were pools of melted silver.

But Gertie's curiosity got the better of her. She wanted to see where Bea would take this.

She squeezed her eyes shut, moaning as Bea's fingers circled and stroked the area in a wavelike motion, teasing her. One finger slipped inside, and Gertie gasped as another hand gripped her jaw. Eyes snapping open, she stared at their reflection. A menacing, dark expression surfaced on Bea's face, one that contrasted with her sultry smile.

Her voice was an unrecognizable growl when she spoke. "Watch the face you make while I'm fucking you."

Ho-ly shiiiiiiiiit. Gertie gulped, fear prickling the back of her throat, and the wetness between her thighs grew slicker as Bea's fingers played with her. Gritting her teeth, Gertie propped herself up on the counter, groaning. With her spare hand, Bea pulled down the top of Gertie's dress, exposing her breasts. Gertie gasped as Bea's hand grabbed onto one, massaging it. To be dominated like this felt humiliating.

She wanted more.

"Shit," Gertie hissed through clenched teeth. Sweat had gathered on her brow, and her curls were beginning to frizz. "B-Bea."

"Want me to stop?" Bea's fingers thrust into her harder, each movement pulsing through her body with a pleasurable violence. Gertie bit her lip and moaned, moving against her hand. Wet kisses graced the back of her shoulders. "Tell me what you want."

"I-I want..." Bea tugged at her underwear again, and it finally fell to her ankles. She teetered on her heels, knees trembling. "I want you to—"

"Yeah?" Bea asked, her pace increasing. Gertie yelped, her voice shifting in pitch. Bea's hand moved from her breast to her ass, smacking it. "Eyes open."

Gertie gasped. "Fuck me."

As Gertie's voice begged for sweet relief, her cries climbing louder, Bea smiled. "Your wish is my command."

Six

Now in the car, Gertie used wet wipes to clean off the sweat gathering under her chin and around her neck. Bea had ordered a car with a partition between the backseat and the driver's, granting them some privacy.

Gertie examined herself in her compact mirror and fluffed up her hair. "Last time I *ever* ask you to zip up my dress."

Bea grinned.

"Don't *smile!*" But Gertie found herself doing the same. "If you walk in smiling like that they'll know exactly why we're late."

"We're getting married. I think they can give us a pass."

Half an hour later, the car pulled up outside the venue, a sprawling estate that had served as the original home of the first mayor of Appledale. Bea climbed out of the car first and held open the door for Gertie, then took her hand to help her onto the sidewalk. Like sardines, they swam through the front doors with the rest of the partygoers, before finally entering the large ballroom space.

By this point in their relationship, the two had an agenda. First: get booze. Second: mingle and schmooze. Third: snoop. After Bea fetched them a couple of drinks, they said hi to their colleagues and friends, accepted more congratulations from people who hadn't learned the news about their engagement, and attempted to field answers to questions they didn't know, like the date and where it would take place.

"People know that kind of thing before they propose?" Gertie whispered to Bea. "Because the way people are looking at us for saying 'We don't know...'"

"Beats me. I thought weddings took like a year or more to plan. When they aren't shotgun ones, that is."

"Yeah..." Gertie's mind drifted back all those years ago to her first one. "Jack and I had been kicking around the idea for the last semester of school. It was a spur-of-the-moment decision. We went to the courthouse when we had our documents and did it for fun." She laughed. "We had no business being married that young."

"Neither one of us did." Bea tucked a curl of Gertie's behind her ear, smiling.

"It would be easier to think of a venue if we had a hobby that we shared. Like hiking or something. Then we could get married in a pretty park."

"Our only hobbies are fucking, talking shit, and watching bad cable TV."

"Hey! We do charity work too!"

"But that's not one of your *favorite* things to do with me is it?"

"Hmm, no, shit-talking probably takes the cake."

"*Bitch!*"

Gertie burst out laughing as Bea grabbed her around the waist, giving her a tight squeeze.

"Behave," Bea teased.

"Why would I want to?" Gertie grinned. "You've shown me what happens when I misbehave…"

At that moment, Gertie spotted a glimpse of something purple and flowy. She turned to see Heather Harrelson, state senator, waltzing by. The woman gripped her husband's arm as they walked along. Her smile, full of perfect white teeth, was dazzling, but her dress was bizarre: puffy lantern sleeves and a flimsy skirt that looked as thin as a dish towel. Knowing these people, though, that ugly ass thing probably cost a cool three grand.

"That's Heather," Gertie whispered. "Heather Harrelson."

"Oh. You want to go say hi?" As soon as Bea said this, she was called over by someone else they knew.

Gertie waved her hand. "Go ahead. Let me talk to her first."

Grabbing her skirt in one hand, Gertie sucked in a deep breath, and made her way to Heather. Nervousness churned within her stomach, tingling all of her nerves. Kayle had completed the research per her request, but because she had gotten distracted by sex, she had been too busy fixing her appearance to review the notes.

Well, fuck it. We're here, aren't we?

For several moments, the woman did not acknowledge her presence, instead continuing to converse with others. *Fucking rude,* Gertie thought, but kept her smile plastered across her face. Eventually, Heather glanced in her direction, and for the briefest of seconds, her smile faltered and her pupils widened with recognition, before regaining its levity.

One thing was clear: she knew Gertie already, and didn't like her.

"Heather, it's lovely to meet you," Gertie said, trying to make her voice sound as chipper and nonthreatening as possible. Pitching it up this many octaves was going to be rough on her voice, though. She reached out a hand to try to shake Heather's, but the woman wouldn't let go of her husband's arm. She laughed in response, and with the hand that clenched her wine glass, gently brushed her fingers against Gertie's, as though she was afraid to touch her for longer than a few seconds.

"I'm so sorry." Heather's voice was as rich and regal as an old church organ. "I don't think we've met."

"I'm Gertie Burns. I'm a member of the Lake County school board. From Appledale."

"Oh, right." Heather's smile stretched a bit too tight. She finally let go of her husband's arm, and the bland-looking man wandered off like a dog without a leash. "I've heard about you! Your election had the highest instance of voter turnout for a school board member the county had ever seen. Impressive."

Impressive when you have a shit ton of money and time on your hands. "Yes! I'm proud my community showed up for me in such a big way."

"I'm sure," Heather said in a tone Gertie couldn't quite place. The woman took a sip of her drink, careful not to smudge her lipstick. Aside from her dress, she was flawless from top to bottom. Gaunt face, high cheekbones, peachy airbrushed skin. "So, planning on making any bids tonight?"

"Oh, no," Gertie said, laughing. "Only a donation."

"How nice. I've got a nine-year-old at home, and there's a custom dollhouse up for auction tonight I've got my eye on. Missed one of her choir performances—hoping this will smooth it over. You know how it is."

No. Gertie didn't. She hadn't missed a single performance of June's, not even in the years after Jack's passing, when she'd been too depressed to leave her bed. No matter how much she loved her work in the PTA and even in the school board, nothing had been more important to her than June. She didn't know how to respond to this, so she took another sip of her drink.

"Are you here with your husband?"

"Nope." Gertie gestured to Bea, who was bouncing among the crowd, life of the party as always. "With my fiancée."

"You're... Oh." Her smile was polite, but there was something venomous in her eyes. By now, Gertie knew what that look meant. *Dyke.* "Oh, you have a...girlfriend? That's a woman?"

Gertie didn't know how to answer that question. Bea had a complicated relationship with gender, and while she used she/her pronouns and liked being called "girlfriend", sometimes she referred to herself as a "dude", "bro", or on her most confident days, a "macho man". Still, Heather's tone offended her. The way she said "*woman*", like Bea was a disgusting example of one, caused her shoulders to stiffen. Woman or not, Bea was a gorgeous person, undeserving of such vitriol. She was the best dressed bitch at this fucking thing, something Heather clearly knew nothing about.

"Yep, that's her." Gertie gritted her teeth behind a closed-mouth smile.

"Oh..."

"Um, I've been following your career for a few years now. I'm amazed at how you've handled some complicated fiscal issues, and with the Lake County budget, I've been hoping I could pick your brain for a few things, if you were open to it? I'd love to have your expertise. I'm also interested in running for the state senate in the future, perhaps a couple years down the line."

Heather sloshed around the liquid in her glass, and her lips screwed together in a smug smirk. "You know, that's quite soon to be running for the state senate."

"Sure! But I'm invested in the growth of my career."

"Interesting. Confident answer. But if that's the case, why didn't you run sooner?"

Gertie stared at her. Heather chuckled, like it wasn't some nasty diss, but an inside joke the two of them shared.

"Maybe if you'd been on the school board for a few years already, I'd say you're ready for something like that. It's quite ambitious to not serve one full term in your current position before running for the senate."

"Oh, I have other administrative and legislative experience. I was the president of the Trinity Oaks PTA for four years—"

"That's cute, but a private school PTA isn't representative of an entire constituency. I admire your ambition—and I'm happy to help you talk through budget stuff—but I assure you, hon, the government is not going anywhere anytime soon, unless the anarchists stage a coup."

"Um... Sure," Gertie said, unsure of how to reconcile being offended with how much she needed her help. "Want to chat sometime next week? I could treat you to coffee, if you'd like."

"You can email my office. It's on my website." Heather offered her one final, killer smile before disappearing into the crowd.

For the first time since she was seventeen, the snide comments of another woman made her feel like crying.

Seven

"**E**XCUSE ME, BEAUTIFUL, IS this seat taken?"

After being so smugly dismissed by Heather, Gertie had retreated to a table toward the back of the room and helped herself to a plate of hors d'oeuvres. Bea had finished her rounds of cajoling with friends, rosy cheeked and bright eyed.

"Bacon-wrapped date?" She tried to smile, but the corners of her lips wouldn't turn.

Bea opened her mouth and Gertie popped it in, giggling at her moans of satisfaction. "Good god, they went all out with the catering here." She pulled out a chair and took a seat, then rubbed Gertie's hand. "I take it that talking with Heather didn't go well?"

"No."

"I'm sorry. I should've come with you."

"No, you were right *not* to." Gertie scanned the room, looking for Heather, but then remembered she didn't give a fuck. *Homophobic fucking bitch with the fake ass veneers.* "I get the feeling she doesn't like carpet munchers."

"Her loss." Bea ate another date. "These are *so* good."

Gertie took a sip from her drink, lost in her frustration. Bea's fingers slipped underneath her chin, turning her attention to her. Gertie swallowed a lump in her throat. Gertie's heart was a hunk of metal, Bea's touch the magnet: no matter how gentle her fingers were, she was moved raucously.

"Fuck her, Gert. You don't need her. You make your own way, come hell or high water."

Gertie sighed. "Hell first."

"Easier to blaze a trail when your last name is literally Burns."

"She said it was too early for me to think about the senate. I'm going to be forty soon. What, am I supposed to wait until I'm a decrepit little geriatric hobbling around on a walker?"

"*Hey.* You would be the cutest little geriatric. And not that it would take you that long to get a position in the state senate, but you could do it if that's what you wanted."

"Oh good god, Bea, I don't want to be doing this past sixty-five. We'll have better things to do." Gertie chugged back more of her drink. "It's not like I want to be president. The state senate feels like an attainable goal. I've got the skills for the job, and more than enough money to fund the campaign, and yet... It's like everyone doubts me. At least when I was on the PTA, people may have hated me, but they still saw me as talented."

"Every bitch with a bad haircut and an ugly ass husband doubts you, which last I checked, is the woman in the room with a gaudy purple dress that looks like a grandma's negligee."

"You said it, not me."

Bea brushed a hand against her face. "People want to tell you that you can't succeed because they're afraid of you. You made people show up for a *school board* election, Gertie. A *school board election*. You've got these motherfuckers shaking in their Armani shoes. You've made countless contributions to your community. *You* did that. Not that asshole."

"I didn't read the file Kayle sent. Maybe that would've helped."

"If she doesn't like *me*? No. Reading a book report wouldn't have helped. Don't make yourself palatable to people who hate you. In two years, when you're ready to run, she'll be eating those words. Make her choke, then swallow."

Gertie smiled. "When did you get to be so tough?"

"When you gave me a leg to stand on." Bea extended her hand. "Come on."

"What?"

"You're too gorgeous to sit here at the back of the room. I gotta show you off."

Gertie slipped her hand into Bea's and allowed herself to be whisked away from all her problems.

"How did I let you talk me into that?"

Gertie untied the ribbons around her heels, freeing her ankles from their tyranny and unveiling the red welts beneath. She threw her shoes to the side, and placed her feet on Bea's lap. Her thumbs began to massage the tender flesh. Relieved hisses escaped Gertie's clenched teeth.

Bea chuckled. "I didn't talk you into anything; I said we should get drinks again and you said—"

"'I love this fucking song,' yes, I know. I'm a sucker for Cyndi Lauper."

"Now I know."

"You overworked me in more ways than one tonight." Gertie sighed. "But if you play your cards right, I might have it in me for one more tango. I'll even let you lead again."

Bea arched her brow. "Ohh... Really?"

"If you're up for it."

"Without question," Bea replied. "Now if only our driver would hurry up..."

Gertie's heartbeat skipped at the growl in her voice. This was an exciting first for them. Gertie loved topping—she liked the power that came with it, the visuals and sounds of Bea losing her mind—but she'd be lying to herself if there weren't days she wished Bea would rail her.

And now, she no longer had to wish for it.

The driver barely pulled to a stop when they exited the car, giggling as they staggered into the house and up the stairs. Stumbling through the door of their bedroom, Gertie pressed her lips against Bea's neck, unable to wait any longer. Bea's hands in turn pulled at the zipper of her dress, and Gertie gasped in delight when the fabric ripped at Bea's desperation. The dazzling garment collapsed to the ground in a heap. As Bea grinned, Gertie's knees quaked.

Bea's hands unhooked her bra and Gertie gasped as she squeezed her breasts with a possessiveness that hurt—and she liked the way it hurt. Squatting down, Bea picked her up, and Gertie yelped with surprise.

"*Beatrice!* You can't lift me! You're going to hurt your back, you're going—"

Gertie squealed with laughter as her lover tossed her onto the bed, crawling on top of her.

Bea stroked her bottom lip with her thumb, inching close for another kiss, but not granting one. "Takes a lot more than that to break me, baby."

Gertie smirked. "I know that. I've broken your back *many* times."

"Yeah. Now it's my turn."

Her hands grabbed Gertie's Spanx, yanking it down along with her underwear. Gertie gasped at the roughness, her excitement ever-growing. She whined as Bea planted kisses on the insides of her thighs, teasing her. Silver eyes glanced up, sparkling with mischief. Licking her lips, Bea returned to the task at hand, much to Gertie's delight. Panting, Gertie grinded her hips against Bea's face, moaning as Bea's fingers slipped inside of her. Although the sensation was pleasant as always, tonight Gertie was impatient. She writhed, toes curling in the sheets, pleasure swelling inside of her, but unable to burst.

She shuddered in frustration. "Bea, I can't—I can't wait any longer."

"Well... Wouldn't want to keep you waiting."

Gertie waited for Bea to return with the strap-on. When she exited the closet, she was still tightening the harness around the waist. Once it was in place, Bea grabbed their bottle of lube from the nightstand, and squirted some onto it. Gertie's chest heaved, watching as Bea stroked the cock. The strap-on had a shorter dildo which penetrated the user, but the receiving end was longer, and would go in deeper. Honestly, Bea was a champ, because looking at this thing now, it looked capable of impaling a bitch.

"Ready?" Bea asked her, lowering herself between her hips.

Gertie nodded, her words failing her in that moment, but her body—oh, her body did not. As Bea pushed inside of her, she gasped, delighted, moaning as a pleasurable fullness filled the lower half of her body. Her hips bucked against her, all-too-eager.

"Easy," Bea whispered, kissing her neck. "We've got all night."

Gertie didn't want to go easy. As Bea's hips moved, she begged her to pick up the pace. They hadn't even turned on the vibrator yet, and this thing felt *this* good? Best ninety-five bucks she'd ever spent. Her hips rocked against Bea, gasping for air, feeling every single button in her body being pressed, but nothing was as in-credible as staring up at Bea's face. God, those eyes, taking her in, excited to ravage her...

...she finally understood why Bea enjoyed being on the receiv-ing end of violence during sex. She wanted it deeper, wanted the aggression, wanted Bea to completely lose it as she had in their bathroom.

"Bea," Gertie whispered. "Hold up a second. Let's try it from behind."

Bea nodded, pulling out. She waited for Gertie to roll onto her hands and knees. She entered her again and Gertie groaned, pressing her face against the mattress. After a few experimental thrusts, Bea spanked her and Gertie moaned again, begging for another. The pace increased, Bea smacking her ass every few thrusts, Gertie crying out in response, her pleasure building to the point of being overwhelming.

But then something happened. They were too close to one side of the bed, Gertie shifted because of her knees cramping, and Bea hit her a little too hard, sending her off balance—

—and she slipped, her head colliding with the edge of their nightstand.

"Gertie!"

Gertie winced, all buzz from their sexual interaction instantaneously gone. Black spots danced in front of her vision. *Goddamn it, this was the problem with silk sheets. Too fucking slippery.* Groaning, she rubbed her forehead. Her fingers grew damp and sticky with blood, but the cut itself wasn't too large or deep. Bea yanked her away from the perilous edge, sitting her upright, cupping her face in her hands.

"Baby? Baby, are you okay?"

"It's...fine," Gertie grumbled. Bea's frantic hands tried to examine her wound but she gently pushed them away. "Bea, I'm fine. We can get back to it."

Bea shook her head. Gertie stared at her, confused. Gone was that (delightfully murderous) sultry look, and instead there was...fear. Nothing but fear.

"We should stop." She ran her fingers through her hair. "I didn't even ask you if it was okay; I shouldn't have hit you like that."

"That's not—that's not a part of our boundaries. We don't ask each other things before we do them. We say 'no' or 'stop' but keep going otherwise."

"When it came to *you* topping *me,* yes. But I shouldn't have... I shouldn't have put my hands on you." Bea undid the straps of the harness in a frenzy, and Gertie stared at her, confused.

"What's wrong?" Gertie asked. She was triggered by *something,* she knew that much. "Do you want to talk about it?"

"No. We just—I'm sorry, we shouldn't have done this. It was a bad idea, and I don't want to do it again."

"*Ever?*" Gertie asked, incredulous. When Bea nodded, she stammered in confusion. "But—why? You got a little carried away with spanking my ass; you didn't commit a crime."

"That doesn't matter." Bea's shoulders trembled. "If I can't control myself, I can't do this. I'm not supposed to—I'm not supposed to act this way."

Those words made Gertie's stomach gurgle with nausea. When she was a child, Bea was abused into subservience, so maybe in some sick way, playing a submissive role was comfortable for her. Predictable. Maybe Bea didn't want to think of herself in the same way as her abusers. Maybe Bea believed that by aligning herself with submissiveness, she could avoid perpetuating harm. And maybe, even accidentally and in a small way, her worst fear came true tonight.

"Beatrice..." Gertie whispered, placing a hand on her knee. "Of course we don't have to keep having sex, but can you please tell me what's wrong?"

"Can you stop asking me about it?" Bea snapped, withdrawing from her touch.

"But you were having fun before, weren't you?"

"For fuck's sake, Gertie, drop it."

Gertie was shocked by the harshness of her tone, the coldness of her eyes. This was a side of Bea she wasn't used to. But at this moment, Gertie didn't feel angry, she felt helpless. Yell at her, and she'd be terrified. Push her, and she'd get more upset. She loved Bea. But loving someone who had been hurt so much was like walking around with a ticking time bomb in the center of her chest. It ticked whenever Bea mentioned something fucked up about her past; when Gertie saw that little girl with the dead eyes in those photos. Sometimes the sympathetic rage she experienced would build up to the point of explosion, as it had with Westley and her parents. But despite the bloodshed, the feelings never went away completely.

She didn't know if they ever would.

Gertie watched as Bea entered their bathroom, slamming the door shut with uncharacteristic anger. Swallowing her dejection, Gertie reached for her phone. Navigating to her email, she opened up the email she received from Kayle about Heather. At the top, in bold letters, it said:

Liberal but homophobic. Lamented the Obergefell v. Hodges ruling and said it was setting a dangerous precedent for state's rights.

Gertie tilted her head backward and sighed so aggressively she hoped her lungs would collapse in on themselves.

Eight

THE BED WAS COLD when Gertie awoke the next morning. When she saw Bea's drool-stained pillow was missing its occupant, her heart sank.

Pushing off the duvet, Gertie yawned and stretched. She picked up her phone, scrolling through her calendar and to-do list. She didn't have any major meetings until 7 tonight, so she didn't need to go to the office. Though based on last night, it might be better to hide out there until Bea got out of whatever funk she was in. She couldn't shake the feeling she had royally fucked up. She had gotten so used to them being in sync that this had rocked her world a bit.

And unfortunately, not in a hot way.

"Morning."

Gertie looked up and saw Bea standing in the doorway. She was dressed in a tank and comfy joggers, a combination which highlighted every muscle and curve her body had to offer. In her hands she held a mug of steaming coffee. She extended it to Gertie like a peace offering, a sheepish smile on her face.

"Permission to speak?"

Gertie arched her brow as she took the mug. "I'm listening."

Bea nodded, swallowing a lump in her throat. "I was a dick to you, and I'm sorry."

Gertie cupped her hand over her ear.

"I was a dick to you, and I'm sorry," Bea repeated, louder.

"Thank you." Gertie took a sip.

"You got hurt, and I—I made it all about me. That was shitty."

"It was." Gertie sighed. "But I get why you were upset; I was being pushy. If you weren't having fun, you weren't having fun."

"But I was! Gertie, I was." Bea crossed over to the bed and sat down. "Before you hit your head, I was... God. That's a side of you I've never seen before, and it was awesome."

Gertie smiled. "Right back at you. And hey, I loved the spanking, for what it's worth."

"Even though I hurt you?"

That same odd expression from last night clouded her eyes again. Gertie rubbed her shoulder, trying to reassure her. *Oh Bea, what the fuck happened? What's going on in that head of yours?*

"I think we simply need more practice, and possibly change up our boundaries?"

"What do you mean?"

"I know we're normally into non-con, but maybe I could try giving you permission to do things? Just until you feel more confident." Gertie's lips grazed against her ear, voice low. "How would it make you feel if I begged you to hit me?"

A blush brightened Bea's cheeks. "Uh, yeah, we can definitely try that."

Bea grasped her hand, pressing a kiss to her knuckles. Gertie set her mug of coffee on the nightstand and giddy, scooted over to her. She planted kisses on her face and jaw, her hands running down her chest.

"If you want, we can wrestle for it."

Bea laughed. "You think you could win?"

"I may not have muscles but I do have *one* advantage." Her manicured nails pricked her skin, tickling her, and Bea squealed with laughter, tackling her against the mattress. Gertie's heart throbbed within her chest as Bea hovered over her, pinning her wrists above her head—*yes, yes, yes*—there was that look from last night, and her grip was so rough her joints ached, and—

"Ack!"

The two looked over to the doorway to where June stood, red-faced, still in her pajamas. She had her phone in one hand, and the other was shielding her eyes.

"You guys know your bedroom door was open, right?"

"We know *now*," Bea said, and Gertie chuckled, burying her face in her hands to hide her embarrassment. "What's up?"

Now certain she wouldn't witness her mothers' sexual escapades, June waved her phone. "Someone posted a TikTok of you last night from the dance."

Gertie had gone viral.

Well, Gertie and Bea dancing at the gala had gone viral, to be precise. Sitting at the kitchen table, they peered down at the phone with skeptical eyes. The video started shaky as it attempted to zoom in and focus on them at the edge of the crowd. Bea twirled Gertie, and her dress shimmered under the lights. As Bea leaned in to whisper something to her, Gertie threw back her head in silent laughter. The caption read, "Me and who when?"

The comments on TikTok, of which there were hundreds, stretched on endlessly.

> *Oh my Goddddd they're so cute I want to die*
> *Why can't someone love me like that*
> *Because you won't get off your phone bitch are you serious lol*
> *What's their IG*
> *Lmao their IG what about their OF*
> *Stop fetishizing lesbians*
> *I am literally gay???*

Finally, in the throng of horny chaos, a commenter emerged to provide some clarity.

> *This is Gertie Burns and her girlfriend. She's a school board member in Appledale*
> *What's her IG???*
> *Humbly also asking to know because my god is she gorgeous*
> *Ughhhh we are unworthy*

Swallowing a nervous lump in her throat, Gertie opened her other social media pages. Her Instagram followers had climbed up by the 1000s, with countless notifications posted on her self-ies and profile pictures—she didn't post Bea online because she didn't like being on social media. Some commenters expressed outrage at this, demanding to see photos of her lover. Others fawned over her beauty.

"There's a hashtag, see?" June, who was hovering over the table, pointed to the caption. "#gertiebea and #gertieburns. That'll show you other videos."

The videos hadn't climbed as fast in view count as the original one that had gone viral, but others were. There had to be at least fifty of them, and every time Gertie refreshed the page, new ones appeared.

Who in the fuck posted that? Gertie navigated back to the original video, and clicked on it. The poster was Emily Branson—the daughter of Richard Branson. She clicked on the previous video the girl had uploaded, a fit check. The girl twirled around in an off-shoulder pink taffeta dress studded with sequins. She looked a little younger than June. Cutie. Shame her dad was such a prick. Probably posted this to piss him off. Despite the violation of her privacy, that had earned a little bit of Gertie's respect.

"What is 'Mother is Mothering'? What does that mean?" Gertie asked.

June chuckled. "It means you're a queen. You're like this super sexy boss lady."

"*Sexy?*" Gertie squinted at some of the comments. "I'm old enough to be the mother of seventy-five percent of these peo-ple."

"Moms can be sexy! God, it's like you never watched *Modern Family*."

"What?"

"Sofia Vergara? *Modern Family*? It was on for years?" When Gertie stared blankly back at her, June sighed, and turned to River. "You have to promise me you'll keep them up to date on pop culture after I'm gone. They're already so far behind."

"That would require *me* to keep up with pop culture," River said.

"This family is impossible."

The kids then dispersed to their respective activities for the day: River, to go practice soccer drills with Holland, and June off to Urban Outfitters with her friends. Gertie continued to scroll through the countless videos, all voyeuristic and strange. After being neglected as a child, she had pursued attention and the praise of others. Now it seemed like she had it, and it didn't give her the joy she had craved.

"People think I'm...pretty."

"And? What's so shocking about that?" Bea asked, nudging her. "You're a knockout."

"I know what *you* think, but—"

"Gertie, no. Not what I think. Like, objectively. "

"It wasn't always that way."

"Because we grew up in a time where you were considered fat if your stomach was barely big enough to hold your organs in. My Mom said I was fat, and I was a size 6 into my twenties."

"Your mother was also a raging narcissist."

"True."

"I *like* my body now. I do." It had taken a long time—decades and decades—but since she started dating Bea, she fell in love with it, wrinkles and rolls and all. "It gave birth to my baby. It fought off violent men. It—"

"Feels *really* awesome when you're on top."

"Thank you," Gertie said, laughing. "Really? It makes a difference?"

"*Yes.*"

"Fascinating." She chuckled again, but didn't stop wringing her hands. "It's weird to hear other people say that when I've gone my whole life being told what a fat ass I was." She bit her lip. "I think I wanted people to like me before they sexualized me."

"Oh, honey." Bea's hand wove through hers.

"It's so stupid how jealous I still am of you. You make friends so easily. People *love* you. And with me, I've always had to try that much harder." Gertie paused. "Did you ever feel weird about being the popular girl when we were kids?"

Gertie remembered how the girls at recess used to comb their fingers through her hair, admiring its length. Every Valentine's Day the boys would fill her cubby with the sparkliest of cards and best of candies. She had sunkissed skin and trimmed eyebrows and all these kinds of shimmery lip gloss Gertie envied from afar.

"It grossed me out, yeah. A lot of what was...*me* back then wasn't me."

"What do you mean?"

"Um... Well, femininity always felt like this performance I wasn't going to win, right? Mom always thought I could be girlier, so my clothes got frillier. Dad didn't like my low register, so I'd have to change my pitch. In the fifth grade, Mom dropped me off at the hairdresser alone and I got that cute little pixie cut..."

"I remember the one."

"Yeah, well, my uncle complained about it. Said he didn't like it that way."

Gertie flinched. Then she said, "I'm glad I killed your parents."

"I know." Bea cracked a smile.

"I don't have any regrets about that."

"I know." Bea kissed her forehead. "I'm sorry this makes you feel squeamish. It'll blow over."

Except it didn't. As the days turned into weeks, Gertie's work and personal phone were blown up with messages. Her email inbox flooded with fan letters. People made stickers with her face that said *Gertie For President, Gaslight, Gatekeep, Gertie-boss,* and *Bi-conic Gertie Burns.* While she enjoyed the attention, it still skeeved her out. Soon the good was usurped by the bad. She and Bea couldn't go out in public without people taking pictures of them. One teenage girl stalked them through a grocery store to ask for an autograph. When it became clear the attention wasn't dying down, she reconsidered her assessment of Emily Branson. *Stupid little bitch. Why does she think it's acceptable to record people in public?*

Gertie arranged for Kayle to give her a taste of her own medicine. After hacking into her Gmail account, they discovered Emily was—*scandalously!*—in possession of her ex-girlfriend's new girl-friend's nudes. One carefully orchestrated leak later, and Emily was facing child porn distribution charges. Richard stepped down from his position in disgrace to prepare for his child's upcoming court date. This allowed Gertie, Winnie, and Laura to seek an appropriate candidate who could usurp his position in the next special election.

Over the course of the next few weeks, they figured out Gertie's old colleague from PTA, Norah Nguyen, lived in Branson's district. She was the teacher chaperone, and by far the most agreeable (and competent) person within that group. After twelve years of teaching, Norah was sick of those shit-ass high school kids. It took little to no convincing to get her to run for office, especially when she had Gertie's support. The three women rejoiced in having found someone who would help them reduce the boys' club, and as Winnie so aptly put it, "Get shit done."

And Gertie was more than happy to do that.

Nine

WHILE IT WAS TOO late for Emily's video to be taken down, eventually good attention surfaced: specifically, from Zoya Faraj, the other state senator that Gertie admired. One night on her way home from a board meeting, she received a call.

"Is this Gertie Burns?"

"Speaking."

Zoya introduced herself. She had a certain cadence to the way she spoke, tactful and rich. If her voice was honey, it would be poured into bottles and sold at Erewhon. Ecstatic, Gertie arranged a date and time to meet for lunch, then had Kayle compile a report. She spent the next couple of nights memorizing it. Zoya was a devout Muslim, Ivy League educated, and also a staunch queer ally; she had marched in a pride parade with her daughter last year. Two days later, Gertie showed up at the restaurant in a nice pair of heels and a business-professional dress.

Zoya dressed modestly yet fashionably. Her floral print hijab was tied in a Parisian knot below her chin. She wore a simple black blouse with full length sleeves, wide-legged slacks, and tan suede boots. When she smiled, she showed dimples and perfect white teeth. Laugh lines rounded the edges of her lips. But what impressed Gertie most were her hands. Weathered, stretching lines expanding across the canvas of her palms. Their roughness contrasted with the delicacy of her long, manicured fingers: the sign of a high class woman who wasn't afraid of hard work.

"Hey there," she said, pulling Gertie in for a hug. *A hug? Holy shit.* "You look lovely! It's so nice to meet in person."

They entered the restaurant and sat in a small booth near the back. The waiter was prompt in bringing them their waters.

Zoya took a sip with a satisfied smile. "Thank you so much for meeting me. I've been so excited to talk to the woman who has been blocking all those obnoxious book bans. And cleaning up some of the budget." She rolled her eyes. "I used to be on a school board, and let me tell you, it was a mess."

"It really is, isn't it?" Gertie chuckled. "Always happy when someone acknowledges the work I've done. Lately all anyone seems to ask me about is my fiancée." Gertie winced. "Um, I'm worried that the TikTok video has...made me seem unserious."

"I don't think so..." Zoya squinted at the menu. "This is good attention. Love is a positive thing, and you not only love your fiancée, but you love your community. That's what I wanted to talk to you about."

"Yes." Gertie's heart was pounding so hard it burned up the back of her throat—or that could've been acid reflux, she wasn't sure. "I, uh, don't know if you know this, but there's a senate seat opening up in the next couple of years. The incumbent is stepping down."

"Well aware." She smiled. "And I know you're interested in it." She folded her hands in her lap. "What I've seen from this social media situation and from studying your career is that you have a way to mobilize people. You're not extroverted, but you've worked to build good relationships. Based on this, Gertie, I think within a decade, you could be one of the most powerful women in Ohio."

"T-Thank you. I'm glad you think so. But could a viral video really translate into votes?"

"*Ahh*. That right there is proof you need my help. See, I gained popularity through networking with others at charity events and making TikToks and vlogs about them. If you capitalize on a strong social media presence, you'll corner the youth vote."

"You—you want me to win?" Heather had treated her so coldly that Zoya's warmth and frankness surprised her. "Really?"

"I do. I'm impressed with your tenacity, and I could use another ally. Your politics, for the most part, align with my own."

"Forgive me, but what about Heather Harrelson? Isn't she in the DFL?"

"Heather's a centrist who runs as a Democrat." An anger as acidic as lemon juice dripped into her voice. "I have big plans in mind, and she's not someone who will go to bat for me."

"I...kinda got that feeling when I met her."

"You did?" Zoya arched her eyebrows.

Gertie explained what had happened at the gala. Zoya sat there, her arms crossed, shaking her head the entire time. When Gertie finished the story, she rolled her eyes, exasperated.

"Typical of her," Zoya said. "I'm so sorry that happened to you. For what it's worth, she's given me a lot of microaggressions, too."

"What are you proposing I do?"

"It'd be helpful for us to develop a working relationship. And if you were to run a campaign, I would contribute to it, as well as endorse it. The only thing I expect in return is for you to do the same."

"Well, thank you. But I... I wouldn't need a campaign donation," Gertie mumbled. "I paid for my first campaign with my own money."

"You did? No fundraising or anything like that?"

"No. I'm a multimillionaire." *One who doesn't want to be bought and sold like so many other politicians are.*

"A multimillionaire who doesn't care to make herself any richer by asking other people for money." Zoya tilted her head back, laughing. "I can see why Gen Z just *loves* you."

Bea popped the cork on the new bottle of wine and poured a glass for Gertie. "Here's to new beginnings and new business partnerships."

"Here-here." Gertie clinked her glass against Bea's.

They were sitting at their kitchen table, Gertie's work papers and laptop stretched across the space. Bea had a legal pad and pen beside her. Tonight, they planned on knocking out some details for their wedding. They knew they wanted to marry within a year, preferably before June would go to college.

"Speaking of new beginnings... Have you given any thought to a wedding venue?"

Gertie scrunched up her nose. "I can't think of what would be 'us'. All I know is no churches, no barns. Barns are so 2013."

"I would spontaneously combust if we walked into a church, so glad we're in agreement on that. And I'm not into places that lack air conditioning or smell like hay." Bea drummed her fingers against the tabletop. "You know what would be funny? If we got married in the Chinese restaurant where we met again."

"That *would* be funny." Gertie smiled. "But I think it's too small for everyone we'd have to invite. And I don't know how the Wus would feel about it, either."

"What about your elementary school?"

Gertie and Bea turned to see June through the kitchen archway, refilling her water bottle. When they stared at her blankly, she made a face.

"It's where you both first met? Duh?" She screwed on the lid. "And it's big enough. Hella cute."

The two winced.

"I don't know if we'd want to get married in an elementary school, June."

"It's just a suggestion!" She held up her hands defensively as she exited the room, retreating upstairs. When her bedroom door shut, they looked at each other with disgust, as though they'd tasted something foul.

"No," Bea said.

"Atrocious suggestion." Gertie sighed. "I can't think of any-thing sentimental that would work. Our first date was at that coffee shop—"

"—which closed down, because it was shit."

"You know what our problem is? We're too spontaneous."

"In more ways than one." Bea grinned and stroked her chin, deep in thought. "The most sentimental thing we've shared is our home."

Gertie snapped her fingers. "Wait. Maybe that's it."

"You want to get married in our house?"

"We have a good kitchen setup for catering. The garden will be a gorgeous backdrop. We just hosted a big party here with all of our friends and neighbors—why not a wedding?"

"You sure you don't want something more extravagant?"

She shook her head. "We can make this place look extravagant. Hell, I can have Kayle fix up the garden."

"He'll do that?"

"He's a gardener by trade. Technically. Why not?"

Bea smiled. "I think that's a great idea."

Gertie leaned in to kiss her, and Bea laughed against her mouth. At that moment, her phone buzzed, and Gertie groaned, picking it up.

"Turn off your phone." Bea kissed her again. "We gotta hash this out."

"One sec..." Gertie took a sip from her glass as she fished it from her pocket. She was waiting on Winnie to email her the agenda notes for the next ad hoc meeting, but to her surprise, it was a text. One from a number she didn't recognize.

UNKNOWN

Hello Gertrude. You don't know me, but you're dating my ex-girlfriend. I came across that TikTok of you two. This is strange, but I've needed to get in touch with her for a while, as I have some things of hers I want to return.

"The fuck?"

"What?" Bea leaned over, trying to peek at the screen. "What's wrong?"

Another buzz.

UNKNOWN

I've got some of her kids' things… photo albums… baby pictures.

"Uh…" Gertie passed her phone to Bea. "I guess your ex wants to return some photo albums."

"What?" Bea muttered, her eyes wide. Another text came in and her mouth parted slightly, surprised.

"What is it?"

"She's in the state. She wants to come over and drop them off." The phone clattered onto the table. Bea's hands raked through her hair, her eyes paralyzed with fear.

At that moment Gertie knew they were in for some deep shit.

Ten

BEA FIRST MET MAGIC in the self-help section of a Barnes and Noble, examining LGBTQ+ coming out books. It had been a whirlwind romance, one which convinced Bea to leave Westley for good, and embrace her life as an out-lesbian. Things had gone sour fast, for no more than a few months after they moved in together, Bea found Magic getting railed by two other butches. Traumatizing. So traumatizing that Bea fled to Ohio to live with her shithead parents, and the rest was history.

It should be fucking history.

Gertie furiously scrubbed at the dishes in the sink, imagining the sponge was a pumice stone, and the plates were the nondescript woman's face. Her nails scraped away shreds of red lasagna and she imagined she was separating skin from muscle. Bea paced the floor of their kitchen while Gertie washed the dishes to take her mind off things.

The day they got the text, Bea arranged for Magic to drop off things, but the woman had wormed her way into the situation further, insisting they "needed closure."

"I asked her to drop off the stuff. Even gave her our address so she could mail it. She insisted on coming here in person," Bea had explained to her. "She has the boys' baby pictures. I don't want to lose those forever."

Gertie conceded. She had killed one of those boys, after all. She figured Bea could at least have the photos to remember Trevor by. Hopefully when he was younger and cuter and not a total fuckwad.

Though she doubted he'd ever been cute.

When she learned Magic had refused to do a simple drop off, she had called Kayle, demanding to know *everything* about the bitch. *Her favorite color, her favorite food, the color of the panties she wore last Sunday—whatever you know, fucking bring it to me.* What Gertie knew: Magic Harmony Meadows, born Contessa Bradley, was a white woman ten years older than they were, though it was hard to tell with all the Botox she'd pumped into her face. A self-proclaimed "life coach" who owned a chain of yoga and wellness centers in Kentucky and Tennessee. An out and proud lesbian, she was lauded by many for running a successful business in a treacherous landscape. Bea had a type. She liked powerful women; Gertie knew that. But Gertie was more powerful, and she was going to show this cunt where her place was. The fact she'd tracked Bea down through a ten second TikTok was all the info she needed to conclude this was a dangerous woman.

A knock at the door startled them both. Bea bit her lip and motioned for Gertie to come to the door. With a sigh, Gertie dried her hands and followed her, animosity festering in her stomach like a container of yogurt that had gone bad. Bea gave her hand a little squeeze before they opened the front door, revealing the woman on the other side.

The first thing Gertie noticed was her tight, taut face, with water-balloon lips. Blue eyes that were electrifyingly bright. She was dressed like someone about to go to a wellness retreat, sporting a tight tank top, loose fitting sweatshirt, and black palazzo pants, however, her blond hair was styled in a curly ponytail. Despite her put-together appearance, she reeked of burned quinoa.

She smiled, and it was so stiff Gertie resisted the urge to giggle. Her eyebrows didn't even move. Examining her further, she was painfully skinny. It gave Gertie great pleasure to know even if she hadn't cheated, Bea wouldn't have stayed. That woman loved tits and ass too much to be with this personified coat hanger. It was weird to imagine these two having sex—much less, that this woman would be topping Bea on the regular. Try as she might, Gertie couldn't picture it.

She was grateful for that.

Magic held up a bag. "For you, Bea." She turned to Gertie. "Thank you for having me."

Gertie smiled, but didn't say anything. She took the bag from Magic, her nails scraping against the top knuckles of her hand, and looked at Bea. "I'll set this in the kitchen. You two can sit in the living room." Seemed fitting. Gertie had killed one of Bea's exes there already. If she had to kill another, well, she could. River was out with Holland again, and June was busy with her friends.

But she couldn't get ahead of herself.

When she entered the living room, she saw Bea and Magic sitting across from each other. Bea's normal posture in a seat was wide-legged and relaxed, but here her back was erect and stiff, her hands grasping her knees like she was squeezed in a roller coaster ride seat. Magic's eyes wandered around the room, as if mapping out the entire space.

She looked at Gertie and smiled—or at least, she attempted to. "You have a lovely home."

"Thanks." Gertie sat down beside Bea.

A flicker of confusion crossed Magic's eyes, but she blinked it away. "I wanted to discuss some things with Bea."

"Oh, that's perfectly fine." Gertie squeezed Bea's knee. "Whatever you have to say, you can say in front of me."

"I'd like to hear from Bea what she prefers."

Bea swallowed. "Gertie can stay. This conversation won't take long."

"I came all this way."

"And I wish you hadn't."

Hurt surfaced in the older woman's eyes. She bit her lip, nodding. "I suppose that's what I deserve."

Gag me. Gertie resisted the urge to roll her eyes. She listened as the two exchanged mild conversation. Magic was in town scoping out an additional location for her business. She mentioned coming across the TikTok and that sparking her memory about Bea moving to Ohio, and the things she left behind. Conveniently, she left out the part about how she found Gertie's personal cell number, and why she wanted to be in Ohio in the first place. She then launched into a rambling apology.

"There were things in our relationship that we were lacking, things I knew I needed," she said. "And instead of coming clean and ending things, I hurt you. And for that I'm so sorry."

Lacking.

So it was a sex thing. The woman was too much of a coward to admit that, though. Maybe this whole fiasco was why topping gave Bea anxiety. But Bea hadn't been nervous about Gertie getting bored with their sex life as much as she'd been nervous about hurting her. There was still a missing piece to this puzzle, and it was pissing her off.

Bea stared at the coffee table like the words she wanted to say were written on it. "That's...it? That's all you have to say?"

"Y-Yes," Magic replied, confused. Her gaze softened, or it seemed to. Jesus, Gertie *really* couldn't tell.

"What about convincing me to leave Westley and upending my entire life?" Bea asked, her voice hoarse.

"Beatrice, I didn't 'convince' you to leave him. You did that of your own accord. Maybe you're misremembering, but..." Magic shook her head, and Gertie hated it; hated how this woman was treating Bea like a child. *She cannot be serious.* "And again, while I'm sorry for hurting your feelings, I'm not sorry for getting what I needed. I feel like you owe me an apology for the ways in which you neglected me—not that I'm asking for one. I know you were dealing with a lot back then."

Gertie shifted in her seat, leaning forward, and Bea squeezed her hand as if to hold her back. Tension seeped into Bea's body, moving into Gertie's. Her heart pounded against her chest and a rawness tore up her throat; a wolf about to howl before the hunt.

"You think I neglected you?"

Magic pressed her hands over her heart. "I can't help how I feel."

Oh this fucking bitch.

"Excuse me for a second," Bea replied.

She exited the room and entered the bathroom beside the kitchen, the tumbling of the lock echoing thereafter. Left alone with Magic, Gertie rejoiced in the opportunity to slam this bitch's face into the coffee table and break her nose, jaw, neck. But she promised Bea she would exhibit restraint.

She crossed her arms. "Now would be a good time for you to leave."

Magic's gaze narrowed. "If you would grant us a moment of privacy—"

"Fat fucking chance."

"Mature."

"Yeah, you would know something about being 'mature', wouldn't you? How old are you? 52? 63? Do you qualify for Medicare?"

"This is between me and her. You have no business treating me this way."

"Uh, yes, I do, because you're a predator that targets newly-out queer women. Probably because you know how to manipulate them into doing what you want."

"What are you talking about?"

"You were looking at coming out books when you met her. You don't think I figured it out?" Gertie squinted at her. "What business would you have had there, as someone who's been out for a number of years?"

She laughed. "I think you're getting too many ideas."

"I wonder how many of your exes would feel that way."

The devastation on Magic's face unveiled like a car crash in slow motion, and Gertie relished every second of it. Her lips twitched, turning downwards, and her brow furrowed.

"Are you a fucking moron?" Gertie asked.

"As I said, I came here to talk to Bea. Not you."

"No, you came here to strong-arm her into talking to you. Do not come into my home and pretend you're so fucking innocent. I see right through it. And so does Bea."

"I've never been spoken to so horrendously in all my life."

"Well, there's a first time for everything. Anyways, when you leave—and I suggest you do that now—you are to stay away from her. Go back to Kentucky where you belong. I am not an enemy you want to make. Understand?"

Magic rose to her feet, hovering over Gertie. "Here's hoping you two will be happy together."

"We were doing fine before you showed up." Gertie shrugged her shoulders, and pointed to the front hall. "Door's that way. Don't let it hit your bony ass on the way out. Your pelvis might break, and I wouldn't want to disappoint whoever's spit roasting you tonight."

She watched the woman leave, and locked the door behind her. Magic took a few steps closer to her Tesla, stopped, and looked back at the house. Gertie flipped her the bird. The older woman rolled her eyes and climbed into her car, then took off down the road. With a heavy sigh, Gertie went to the bathroom door and knocked.

Bea's voice, riddled with tears, echoed back. "Did she leave?"

"Yeah, she left. And I didn't even have to kill anyone this time." Gertie smirked, leaning her head against the door. "You should be proud of me."

Bea laughed, then sniffled. Toilet paper ripped and Bea blew her nose. Gertie slumped against the door. Hearing her lover cry made her heart crumple and crash like an eight car pile-up.

"Talk to me, angel."

"I don't..." Bea wept again. She opened the door, and Gertie gazed into her face. Blotchy, bright red, her eyes an endless water-fall. It was a familiar and heartbreaking sight, one that harkened back to the day Gertie had killed Earl, and came clean about her revenge plot. Something had happened between her and Magic.

Something way worse than cheating.

"Bea, honey..." She pushed into the bathroom, gathering more toilet paper to clean her face. "She wanted to control you. That's all this was."

"I know, I'm sorry. I don't want you to think I'm this upset because I'm not over her or something, I just..."

"I don't think that at all. But did she do something to you? Did she..."

"Gertie, I can't." Bea sobbed. "I can't talk about it."

Fuck. Maybe I should've killed her. Gertie ushered her out of the bathroom and into the kitchen. She helped Bea sit down and fetched her a glass of water.

Bea reached for the bag on the table, pulling out a photo album. It was a hefty leather book with a few streaks of mold on its crumpled surface. Bea cracked it open and peeked inside. She frowned. Flipped to another page. Blinked in disbelief. Flipped to another, then another, beginning to hyperventilate, before finally breaking into sobs once more.

"Bea, what's wrong?"

With an aggravated scream, Bea threw the album at the wall and crumpled, wailing in distress. Gertie picked it up. As she flipped through the pages, fury broiled in her body. It wasn't that the photo album was empty; many pictures were still in it.

Pictures of Bea at her first wedding, pregnant and on the verge of tears as Westley's hand forced her to slice their poorly-frosted sheet cake.

Bea wearing dresses and heels.

Bea pregnant, looking at her belly as though an alien was about to burst from it.

But that wasn't the worst part. Flip another few pages, and she found even worse photos, ones Bea had told her about, and had hoped she'd never see. Judging from the torn pockets and crumpled edges, they'd been jammed in there, and weren't supposed to be a part of this album.

No pictures of River or Trevor. Gertie's phone buzzed, and trembling with rage, she checked her screen.

UNKNOWN

Tell Beatrice I'll give her the pictures back when she agrees to hear me out.

Eleven

"I'm trying to find her, ma'am, but she's gone dark. I'll take a look at the security cam footage you sent me and see if I can run that license plate. Might have a friend who can hack into some traffic cams. Even if the car's a rental, it'd give us an idea of where she's at."

Gertie pinched the bridge of her nose together. "Whatever it takes, Kayle."

"When I find her, you want her alive?"

"Yes." *So I can gut the fucking bitch myself.*

"You got it. Talk to you when I have an update."

With a sigh, Gertie ended the call. She glanced at Bea, curled up underneath the covers of their bed. She had stopped crying hours ago, but was now lying there in a comatose state.

"You want to eat a little something? Soup and crackers? I'll even get you that clam chowder you love."

Bea sighed. *Finally, she made a noise!* "I'm not hungry."

"Okay." Gertie took a deep breath. "Are those the only copies Westley made?"

"No. They're online, too."

"I can have Kayle clean those up."

"I've been trying to remove them for *years,* Gertie. When they're gone from one site, they go up on another." Bea sat up, rubbing her bleary eyes. "Why do you think I only ever worked shitty jobs? Because every time an employer runs a background check on me, they find those photos. Even after I cut off all my hair, I mean it's *clearly* me."

"There has to be something Kayle can do."

Bea shrugged. "Good luck." A pause. "You're going to kill her?"

"I won't, unless you want me to." The words were sharp like thumbtacks as they left her mouth—*Jesus fucking Christ I can't believe I'm saying this*—but she meant them. "Whether she lives or dies, she needs to give you those photos back."

"I wonder if she even has them. Or if she destroyed them to fuck with me."

"Bea, I had no idea she was this bad. I mean, I assumed she was, but this..."

This was the kind of shit Gertie would do to take out an opponent. Actually, this was worse, because even Gertie didn't think she'd use scenes of someone's actual sexual assault. In each of those photos, Bea was being violated in some way. Not only were those images plastered all over the darkest of porn sites, they were seared on the surface of her brain. It was all she could do to keep from crying herself.

Gertie sat on the bed beside her, her voice soft. "Why didn't you tell me? I would've been better prepared to handle her."

"You mean kill her."

"I wouldn't—I could've just beat the shit out of her and sent her on her merry way."

Bea sighed, squeezing her eyes shut. "I've been open with you about a lot of things over the course of our relationship, but there're some things I don't want to talk about, even now."

"Okay. I understand."

Gertie combed her hand through Bea's hair, but she flinched at her touch. Hurt, Gertie shrank away, and allowed herself to fester in her anger toward Magic. She was frustrated by her lack of inaction. A year ago she'd be taking matters into her own hands and wouldn't give a shit about anyone or anything—but a year ago she wasn't in love with Bea.

Things were different now. Different for the better. Even if it would be easy to wrap her hands around that bird-bitch's little throat and strangle her silly, she couldn't. Her actions had consequences not only for her, but Kayle, Bea, her kids, all the people around her who cared for her and wanted her to succeed.

It would take every ounce of strength to *not* break her promise.

Two days later, Gertie and Bea attended another event; this time, an awards ceremony for Community Changers, or people in Appledale who had enacted a great amount of social change. Gertie, of course, was nominated, and though she told Bea she didn't have to go, Bea insisted.

They'd been unable to track down Magic's whereabouts. The bitch probably knew she had pissed off the wrong person, and was deep in hiding. Kayle managed to locate the hotel where she was staying, and had someone posted there, but they hadn't found her yet. At this point, they had to play a waiting game.

Predictably, Gertie won the award. With a big smile and rosy cheeks, she walked onstage to accept the award and give a rousing speech about how much she loved Appledale. Which, meh, she more so loved how Appledale loved her rather than the town itself, but close enough. Once offstage, she hugged Bea and kissed her cheek, and the two were whisked away to speak with the press, further from the throngs of people and tables. This event, which would normally be a blip in the town newsletter, was now a big deal in their post-viral life.

She answered questions for journalists, most of whom wanted to know about upcoming school board issues, which she answered in detail. She was growing tired, wishing for another cocktail, when she noticed a journalist withdraw their phone. As they glanced at the screen, their eyebrows arched in surprise. While Gertie continued to speak to the reporters, she noticed how this person was turning around and whispering something to the others, pointing to whatever was on the screen. One by one, they all began to check their phones. Confused, Gertie reached into her purse and checked her phone for alerts, finding one from the local paper.

CONVICTED CHILD RAPIST ORIGINALLY SENTENCED TO 40 YEARS TO BE RELEASED ON PAROLE.

Gertie's throat swelled shut. With her heart hammering in her chest, she looked at Bea, who had also picked up on what they were doing, and had checked her phone as well. Devastation spread across Bea's face, the peachy color fading to ash like the aftermath of a wildfire. Looking at the journalists and how their eyes laser-focused on Bea, Gertie knew they were making the connection. Whispers coursed through the crowd, jaws dropping in simultaneous shock. They raised their hands, their voices gaining in volume.

Gertie's voice hardened to steel. "Questions are over."

They clamored for her attention, but she ignored them. Taking Bea's arm, she guided her to the exit. As they passed by the various tables, the murmurs of the crowd filled their ears. Bea's shaking legs wobbled beneath her as some of the reporters tried to call them back over. They exited the venue, descending the steps, reporters close behind them, beckoning to Bea.

"Bea?" Somehow Gertie's voice finally cut through the din. "Honey, are you okay?"

Bea gulped down air. "No."

A familiar buzz echoed. With a sinking sense of dread, she checked the message on her phone.

UNKNOWN

It's not nice to keep a gal waiting.

Twelve

GERTIE HAD NIGHTMARES ON a regular basis. Sometimes she'd see her mother dying in the car crash that transformed her into a human pin cushion for the glass piercing her body. Other times she envisioned losing her battle against Westley. Sometimes there wasn't any violence; she'd see Trevor sneak in through the kitchen side door and that was enough to get her blood pumping. Those were nightmares.

But this—*this?*—there were no words to describe it.

News regarding Bea's uncle was plastered across the front page of the hometown paper, as well as papers in adjacent counties. Not to mention the enormous attention it was garnering on social media. The details were gruesome and invasive, and Bea was beyond distraught. When they got home from the awards ceremony, she crawled into bed and shook the whole night; occasionally threw up.

She didn't want Gertie to touch her.

After she woke up, Gertie contacted her colleagues to inform them she wouldn't be attending her meetings for the next few days. She also had to cancel her regularly scheduled lunch with Zoya.

"I'm so sorry," Gertie said. "I need to help her get through this."

"Do not apologize to me. Family is *always* more important."

When Gertie hung up the phone, she swallowed hard. *Family is more important.* And to protect her family, Gertie would do anything. She already called Kayle to start a smear campaign against the journalist who had broken the news last night. Bea had carefully guarded her past with her uncle. As a child, she had changed schools, and back then, while her uncle's trial was written about in the news, all the articles back then didn't identify her, only stated her age.

Overnight, Magic had eradicated decades worth of work.

Tiptoeing back into the bedroom, she found Bea, sitting up in bed, face in her hands. Gertie sat beside her, but didn't touch her.

"You know what I think would be great? Pancakes."

"I'm not hungry."

"Honey. You've barfed so much I'm sure you've burned a hole in your stomach. Please, even if it's only a saltine, let's try to get your nausea in check."

"You should go to work."

"What? *No!* I'm not leaving you. They can manage fine without me for a few days."

"A few days? Gertie—"

Gertie pressed a finger to her lips. Bea's eyes narrowed, but Gertie was happy with this little surge of anger. Anger was better than emptiness. Hell, Bea could punch her in the face if she wanted to. If Bea split her lips open she'd lick the blood from them with glee.

"You're more important to me than work. If you want me to not talk to you, that's fine. But I'm not letting you sit in this house alone. So what do you need from me?"

For a moment, Bea's expression stiffened, before it crumpled altogether. Her voice warbled. "I need to be held."

"No problem." Gertie laid on the bed and Bea curled up against her chest. Her tears dampened the front of her shirt, and Gertie stroked her back, trying to soothe her.

This was familiar in the worst possible way.

In the afternoon, Gertie departed the bedroom only to return with four popsicle sticks, cursive writing scrawled on the sides. She clenched them in her fist, holding them out to Bea.

"You know," Gertie said, batting her eyelashes, "I'm hungry, but I can't make a decision about what to eat for lunch. You decide for me."

Bea smirked. "I know what you're doing, Gert."

"I'm doing nothing other than asking you to help me make a decision."

Bea pulled a stick from her hand. *Kyoto Sushi.* One of her favorites. She showed it to Gertie, who nodded, and proceeded to order on her phone.

"I said I wasn't hungry," Bea reminded her, but she couldn't help but smile.

"Well, I don't have to share, do I?"

Bea laughed. Gertie kissed her head and continued adding items to her list. Once their food was delivered, Gertie switched off her phone—it was clogged with emails, texts, and voice-mails. Some of them were apologies and well-wishes from friends, but a lot were media outlets seeking to get a juicy soundbite or quote. *Fucking vultures.*

After grabbing the food from the Uber driver, Gertie brought it upstairs. "I know I've said no eating in bed, because I don't want crumbs, but today I can make an exception."

"That bag is *massive.*"

"I splurged on some extra sashimi."

"Wow. I wish I had mental breakdowns more often."

"Oh, so you *do* want to eat?"

Bea giggled. "I might want a bite, yeah."

"Good thing I ordered enough."

"Yeah, good thing you specifically bought all my favorite rolls."

"Um, rude. Maybe your favorites are my favorites."

"This is an eel roll, and the last time I made you try that, you almost puked."

Gertie shuddered. "What are you talking about? I—I totally love eel."

"You can drop the bit, babe. I'll eat."

Bea cracked open the bag and reached inside for the containers. They sprawled them across the bed in a haphazard disarray, giggling like children, before digging into the meal. They ate and watched Bravo until every single container of food had been cleared out.

"Good?" Gertie asked her. "How's your stomach feeling?"

"Much better." Bea shoved the trash into the delivery bag, then laid back on the bed beside Gertie. She looked over at her, her gaze wary. "So what do you think you're going to do..."

"About..."

"Him."

"Once we take care of Magic, we'll figure out his release date, and arrange for him to take a loooooong trip."

"Gertie, you can't kill him. They'll figure out you did it."

Gertie shook her head. "They won't. Your parents died in a car wreck. No one but Misty suspected me of doing anything to Westley—even then, I don't think she believed I killed him. And Trevor 'ran away from home.'"

"I think if you killed my uncle they'd poke around."

"We can make it look like an accident."

Bea's eyes narrowed. "I said *no*, Gertrude."

"I..." Gertie squeezed her eyes shut and took a deep breath. "I'm sorry. I want you to feel safe. And I'm willing to do whatever it takes to make that happen."

"I know you are. That's why I have to put my foot down." Seeing how dejected Gertie looked, Bea leaned forward and kissed her cheek. "Come on, baby. We agreed the last time there was too much to lose."

"I know. You're right."

A teasing smile crossed Bea's lips. "I'm right?"

"You're right."

"Did it hurt to say that?"

"A little."

Bea giggled and kissed her, which Gertie returned. Bea's lips moved to her neck while Gertie's hands found their place at the small of her back, grazing the soft flesh beneath her tank top. Bea pulled Gertie on top of her, her kisses growing urgent.

"Bea, wait," Gertie said, sucking a deep breath into her lungs. Every part of her was revved up to go, but she exercised restraint. "Are you sure?"

Bea cupped her face in her hands. "I'm sure. I want to feel you. It'll make me feel better."

"Emotionally or physically?"

Bea grinned. "Well if you make me feel good *physically*, the good emotions will follow, right?" She wrapped her arms around Gertie's waist, kissing her neck again. "You—you might want to be gentle, though. I'm not sure I can..."

"So just tongue and fingers?"

"Yeah. Is that okay?"

"Of course it's okay. You're in charge."

"Uh, I think we both know who's in charge here." Bea smirked.

Gertie held up her hands defensively, chuckling. "I can't help it if you love my domineering personality."

"That's not the only thing I love about you." Bea giggled as she removed Gertie's glasses, setting them on their nightstand. "I can think of plenty more."

Gertie wiggled her fingers. "And I can think of five right here."

Thirteen

AFTERWARDS, THE TWO SNUGGLED close together. Gertie smiled as she gazed at her lover's flushed face and rubbed her shoulder. Bea squeezed her tight.

Gertie kissed her forehead. "Feeling better?"

"Much better." Bea's voice came out strange, a cross between a warble and a groggy grunt. "Sorry."

"Why're you apologizing?"

"That had to be boring for you."

Gertie laughed. "Oh my god, Beatrice, I'm not *that* much of a sadist. I like vanilla sex, too. And I don't know if you've noticed, but I *love* going down on you."

"Really?"

"*Yes.* Literally all the fun of topping without exerting as much energy. But you almost never ask me to do it."

"Sorry."

"No need for that." Gertie ran her fingers through Bea's hair. "I know I have a short and chaotic attention span, but I'm never going to get bored with you. All I want is for you to be comfortable asking me for things."

Bea smiled. Gertie held her tight even as the summer heat over-loaded their bodies.

"I like fucking. The knife play, the slapping, the choking? Incredible. But I like making love with you, too. Honestly, any opportunity to see you naked is pretty rad."

"It's just... Sometimes I wonder... Do... Do you ever wish you were with anyone more... Less traumatized? I mean, you could have any woman you wanted."

"No. I couldn't." Gertie smirked. "I don't like most women."

"You don't like most men, either."

"*Hey!*"

"Honestly if you told me you were some flavor of demiromantic, I'd believe it."

"What does that mean?"

"Demiromantic is when you're only attracted to people you have a deep emotional connection to."

"Isn't that normal?"

"No. I've been attracted to you from the moment I met you. You were my gay awakening."

Gertie gaped, eyes sparkling with delight. "I didn't know that!"

"How could I have not? You had those cute little chipmunk cheeks and those beautiful dark curls. Not to mention those *curves.*"

"Back then you told me you hated my hair. You called it a rat's nest."

"Because I was a jealous little shit."

"You really were a little shit."

Bea laughed. "What can I say? But anyways... Think about it, Gert. You've been in love with only two people your whole damn life, and you didn't fall for me until after we had sex for the first time. Up until that point, were you even attracted to me?"

"Um... Hard to say?"

"Okay. What about Jack? Were you attracted to him from the moment you met him?"

"He was sweet! But I..." Gertie trailed off, confused. She hadn't developed feelings for Jack until they had spent a considerable amount of time together. And with Ted Gustafo, the widower she had been set up with for one date, he was handsome, but she felt nothing. Less than nothing, actually. "Whoa."

"Yep."

"I didn't think there was a word for that. I thought I was an emotionally constipated, late-in-life bisexual."

Bea giggled. Gertie stroked her cheek.

"How could you ask me then, if I'd ever want to be with anyone else?"

Bea chewed on her lip, staring up at the ceiling. "Because you're you. You're rich, sexy, successful..."

"Rich because of tragedy. Not because of my own brains or anything."

"But you are smart," Bea whispered. "I mean, shit, Gert. You went to Penn. *Penn.* I got my diploma and went into flipping burgers and stocking boxes in grocery aisles, and when I couldn't escape my parents fast enough, hitched my wagon to the only guy who'd take it. And—*and*—you're a better mom than me."

"What?" Gertie laughed. "What makes you think that?"

"When...you told me what you did to Trevor, I—I didn't feel bad." Bea blinked hard. "I really didn't. And I've *never* protected River like I should have."

"Trevor was a lost cause. He created grief for everyone, and if he hadn't hurt June, he probably would've hurt us. Besides that, you were living in an abusive household. How could you have protected your kids when you had to save yourself?"

"By leaving."

"Without money?" Gertie shook her head. "I might make motherhood look easy, but again: I'm rich. If I hadn't won that lawsuit, God knows how June would've turned out."

Bea fell silent.

"So you think all of that makes you unworthy of me?"

"I mean, kinda! Yeah! Kinda does. You're a real life Mary Sue and I am human garbage personified. Especially when we take into account the arsenal of problems I've caused you—"

"Whoa, whoa, whoa." Gertie pressed a finger to her lips. "Stop." Removed it. "Where is this coming from? And by the way, is it the problems *you* have caused me, or is it the problems bad people in your life have caused me?"

Bea stared at her.

"You didn't choose to be abused by your uncle. You didn't choose to have shitty parents. You didn't choose to be baby-trapped by some asshole. So why do you think you're the problem?"

"I... I don't know. Maybe because I'm the common denominator? I came back into your life, and you had to kill a whole bunch of people just to keep us all safe?"

"Sweetheart." Pain caught in Gertie's throat. "You aren't the common denominator. Abusive people are. Stop torturing yourself over this."

"How could I not?"

"Because I was like this *before* you, not *because* of you."

Gertie had homicidal thoughts and urges long before she started that revenge game against Bea. When her father had shouted at her to use the bathroom by herself and she had cried and pissed her pants, she contemplated sneaking into his room in the night to do a little bloodletting. A slash across the throat, a stab to the kidney, or if she was feeling particularly creative, scooping out his voice box with a rusty garden trowel so he could no longer scream at her. When Jack's high school friends had refused to treat her with respect, she wanted to throttle them against the lockers until their heads cracked open and their brains dribbled down their acne-ridden faces. When a professor berated her in class, she fantasized about visiting his office hours to stab him in the eye with a ballpoint pen.

For a long time, she blamed Bea for these violent tendencies. But they were her own. Her pedigree. Bea's assault and bullying hadn't helped, sure, but Gertie's psychological state was by no means all her fault. A lot more things would've had to go right in their lives. A lot more people would've had to treat them better.

"You sure?"

Gertie sighed. "Trust me." She kissed her nose. "I love you, Bea. You're the only person I could ever love, aside from the guy that's six feet under."

Bea cackled, smacking Gertie's arm playfully. "That's so—that's so rude!"

"Trust me. He'd find it funny, too."

Fourteen

Dinner was uncomfortable. June and River were uncharacteristically quiet, pushing around the food on their plates as though the concept of eating was foreign to them. June kept staring at Bea, her eyes growing wetter by the second, until finally she threw her fork down on her plate.

"Are we seriously not going to talk about it?"

"Talk about what?" Gertie asked.

June flattened her hands on the table, her voice climbing in anger. "The pedophile that's getting released from prison?"

"How did you find out about that?"

"Mom, seriously? *Everyone* in town is talking about it."

Gertie's voice sharpened. "You need to dial it back—"

"Gertie, it's fine." Bea interjected, then looked at June. "What do you want to talk about?"

"Should we be worried he'll come find us and get revenge or something?"

Bea shook her head, wiped her mouth with a napkin. "No, June."

"If he was convicted to forty years, why are they letting him go? How is he eligible for parole?"

"We're looking into it," Gertie said. "But neither you nor River have anything to worry about, okay? You're safe here. No one is coming after us."

"Bea." June's voice caught in her throat, and her eyes filled with tears. Bea flinched. She couldn't stand to see her cry. "Bea, I'm so sorry. I'm so, so sorry."

Christ. What did she learn at school? "Junebug. You need to calm down."

"June." Bea reached across and touched her hand. June squeezed it, tears dripping down her cheeks. "We're safe. What happened back then—it was horrible, but I made it through."

But June was inconsolable, even as she clenched Bea's hand. "You weren't that much younger than me."

A knock at the door startled them. Gertie's eyes widened with rage and she threw down her napkin. "Bastards."

"Gert," Bea said, her voice hoarse. "Ignore them."

Gertie approached the front door, fists clenched, but her anger dissipated when she saw Kayle standing there. He held his hat in his hands, and looked at her with big eyes, like a child that had broken his mother's favorite vase.

"I didn't know y'all were eating," he said. "I can come back later."

"Do you have good news?" she asked him.

He bit his lip and nodded. She sighed and stepped aside to let him in.

"Why don't you fix yourself a plate, then?"

After dinner, Gertie sat outside, listening to the crickets singing. She heard the screen door squeak open and Kayle exited the house, hands damp from washing the dishes. Somehow in the faint light, she could see his skin had an unhealthy pallor, blackness circling the undersides of his eyes like stains left behind by a coffee mug. He hadn't been sleeping.

"Y'all were quiet around the dinner table." He sat down across from her.

She arched a suspicious brow. "Kayle, did you... Did you know anything about this?"

Kayle bit his lip.

"Because it would be a huge violation of my trust and our business partnership, for you to not come to me about these things."

He took a shallow breath. "I... I knew about him getting out soon."

"And you didn't think to mention that, like, at all?"

"I figured I'd carry out the hit before you asked for it to happen, collect the cash later." Anxious, he reached a shaking hand into his pants pocket and pulled out another cigarette.

Gertie stared. "You knew him."

"I..." He swallowed. "Yes."

"Are you related to Bea?"

"No, ma'am. He was my neighbor. Mama used to work nights and when I got to high school I was busy with football, so my little brother... He got locked out of the house one time and went to his place for help. And you can guess what happened next." His hands fumbled with the lighter desperately, and Gertie helped him. "Thank you."

"So that's why you got involved with us. You're not avenging Earl. You're avenging your brother."

"Damn straight."

"So that's why you weren't upset about Earl."

"I'm not upset about Earl because he was a damn old fool," he said, tapping the ash from his cigarette. "You know, when you—well—he and I didn't see eye to eye on that. He believed it was wrong, but I knew why you did it. And I think that's what got me thinking that maybe... Maybe he didn't understand me. Because if he knew the lengths I'd go to in order to avenge my brother, well, I don't know why he didn't understand why'd you defend your daughter by any means necessary."

"And your brother? Where is he?"

Kayle stared back at her with cold eyes. He tapped his cigarette off again and jammed it in the corner of his mouth. Shook his head and sighed. Said everything Gertie needed to know.

"I'm so sorry." She took a deep breath. "So, what's the news?"

"Magic flew back to Lexington this afternoon."

"Great." Gertie sighed.

"You know how you want to take her down?"

"Your files gave me everything I needed to know. I've been working on it."

"Sounds good." He took another drag of his cigarette. "Is that all, ma'am?"

"No." Gertie bit her lip. Tears pricked at the corners of her eyes when she realized what she had to do. "We can't take any more chances right now. I need a report on Bea."

Fifteen

K AYLE'S WARNING HAD SENT shivers down her spine, but Gertie read the report anyway. After reading, she went to find Bea in the garden, where she was fixing some of the sprinklers. She offered her a glass of lemonade, which Bea accepted.

"What's up?" Bea asked, wiping her forehead.

"Can we sit down?"

Bea nodded. They sat at the patio table in silence for several moments, pouring glasses of lemonade and sipping in silence. Gertie laid her palms flat against the tabletop, staring at her fingers as though they shielded tarot cards that predicted how this conversation would go. Bea was going to feel betrayed. She knew that much.

"So...you had a DV charge that got dropped two years ago."

Bea stared at her. "You had Kayle run a report on me?"

"I didn't want to take any more chances—"

"Why didn't you ask?"

"How am I supposed to ask you things I don't know about, Beatrice? You haven't exactly been forthcoming with information lately. And I'm sorry, but we just went to a benefit for a women's shelter two months ago, so bringing someone there who had a domestic assault charge is kinda horrible!"

"You've literally murdered people."

"Look, we agreed after what happened with Earl there weren't going to be any more secrets between us. You've told me about everything else that happened to you, so why is this any different?"

Bea huffed and crossed her arms. She paced across the porch, then stopped, placing her hands on her hips. Gertie sighed, dragging her hands over her face.

"I'm not going to pretend I know everything going on inside your head, Bea. God knows you can't sort out mine. But this is not something you can keep a secret from me. Not when it concerns your safety, and the safety of our family." Gertie gulped down a lump in her throat, her voice hoarse. "From the moment I fell in love with you, all I've ever wanted to do is protect you. But in order for me to do that this time, no matter how hard it is, you—you have to let me in."

Bea sat down again, but kept her eyes averted from Gertie. Her foot bounced against the floor in a quiet drumbeat, and her hands moved to her mouth to pick at her lips. Shreds and slivers of pink skin peeled away.

"I'm not proud of what I did."

Gertie's heart hit her stomach, but she remained silent. Bea swallowed a large lump in her throat, her voice hoarse.

"You know the story of why I ended things with Magic. But you didn't know *how*," Bea said. "I think when I told it to you, I made it out to be like I took off after it happened. But I didn't. I tried to leave, but she wouldn't let me."

"What do you mean?"

"I was upset, bawling. And she told me to sleep on it; that I would be more rational in the morning. Went to bed, and River came to keep me company, and Trevor was...gone somewhere. You remember how he was. When I woke up, the bedroom door was locked. It was on the second floor and there was no escape.

"We were locked up for seven hours. No food or water. I begged her to let us out. She wouldn't hear it. I got scared. So I took a chair and broke down the door, and when she tried to stop me from leaving, I punched her. I left, but she called the cops, and I was brought to the station. She came to pick me up and drop the charges." Bea's eyes watered. "They were going to take River from me. It was the scariest day of my life."

"They didn't believe you?"

"People who look like me don't get the benefit of the doubt." She sighed. "We went back home and she ordered me to be obedient, or she'd have the cops pick me up again. Trevor came home, and in the dead of night, we fled Kentucky." Bea wiped her eyes. "Whether you believe me or not, that's alright. River, he can—he can corroborate. If you need to talk to him, you—"

"Beatrice."

Bea burst into tears. Gertie pressed her head against her stomach, and allowed her to cry. Her lover's muscular arms struggled to wrap around her waist, her body on the verge of exhaustion.

"I thought you wouldn't believe me."

"I believe you," Gertie whispered. "And that's why I have to kill her. A woman like that is only going to get more dangerous."

"*Gertrude.* No. You can't put your hands on her."

Gertie cupped her face in her hands. "What if I told you I didn't have to?"

Sixteen

HALF A CUP OF organic almond milk. A tablespoon of monk fruit sugar. Served over ice, in a glass, with a reusable bamboo straw. Magic prepared her coffee like this every morning. Unfortunately, she forgot to buy more almond milk, meaning she'd have to drink it black.

"Why is my life so hard?" She whined. She opened a cabinet to discover the sugar was missing. "Damn it." Haplessly opened another before deciding on having the coffee over ice. She retrieved a glass, but when she went looking for a bamboo straw, she couldn't find it. Grimacing, she took a sip from her glass, resisting the urge to spit it out. With a heavy sigh, she turned and walked over to her dog's bowl. "Pepper! Breakfast!"

She waited to hear her jingling collar, but—nothing. She called her name again, and still, nothing. Mumbling cuss words beneath her breath, she strode through the house, heels of her boots clicking against the floor like a timebomb. *"Pepper! Pepper!"* She walked into the living room, and screamed, dropping her glass on the floor.

Gertie sat on a chair in the center of the room. One hand held a small glass of orange juice, and also, one of Magic's bamboo straws. From the balcony that overlooked the living room, a single rope, tied in a noose at the end, hung suspended over a chair.

Gertie took a loud sip. "Morning, Sleeping Beauty."

Aghast, Magic stumbled backward, hand clutched to her chest as though she was having a heart attack. Gertie chuckled. *Shit, maybe she'll make this easy for me.* The moron slipped on the puddle of coffee and glass at her feet and Gertie laughed. Scowling, the woman regained her balance, squaring her shoulders.

"Where is my dog? How did you get in my house?"

Gertie took another sip of her orange juice and smacked her tongue against the roof of her mouth in disgust. "Of course you'd be the type to get the *pulpiest* kind. Are you cheap, or do you just have bad taste?"

Magic lifted a shaking finger and pointed it at the noose. "What the fuck is that?"

"Do you need glasses or something?"

Magic sighed, squeezing her eyes shut. She rubbed her temples and muttered some sort of gobbledygook underneath her breath.

"I'm calling the police."

"You can't."

Frowning, Magic pulled out her phone and looked at it.

"Cell phone jammer. No calls going in or out. Wanted to make sure we had the utmost privacy, since that was so important to you the last time."

"I wanted privacy with Bea."

"Tough shit. You're not getting it. And hey, while we're at it, don't think about running or fighting me. I've got a couple guys posted up and down the street, one waiting in the garage... You're not making it out of here."

Magic sighed again. "L-look, what I did was callous, but I mean, think if you were in my shoes. Your ex-girlfriend is getting married less than a year after she left you. And to a woman that... Well..." Her mouth remained in a crisp neutral line, but her eyes ogled her with disgust. Gertie was used to that expression by now.

"So punish her?"

"No, I—"

"Steal the baby pictures of her sons, and replace them with...revenge porn? Then leak the story about her pedophile uncle getting out of prison to the press?"

"I-I didn't leak that story."

"Are you sure about that?" Gertie's eye twitched, but her smile remained. "You know what? You wanted to be the victim in this story, and that's *exactly* what I'm going to do for you. I'm going to give you the full victimhood experience."

Magic stiffened. "Do you have any idea what she's done?"

"Spare me. I already know the details."

"Then you know she hit me."

"You were holding her hostage." Magic's bottom lip trembled, though tears did not fill her eyes. Gertie rolled her eyes. "Cry me a river, you anemic fucking crocodile."

"Do you have any idea how traumatizing that was for me?"

Gertie blinked, shocked, and then she spluttered with laughter, one hand clutching her side. Magic didn't say a word. After what felt like eons, Gertie's guffaws quieted to chuckles.

"This whole fucking time—this *whole* time—I thought her parents and Westley were the problem. But no. It was you. *You're* the one who fucked with her head. You persuaded her to leave her abusive husband, promising to help her, and when you were bored, you cheated on her, gaslit her, and convinced her that she was the villain. You provided a safe space for a vulnerable woman only to rip it away. And you have the audacity to stand here and tell *me* about trauma?" Images of Bea's tearstained face, and a terrified River, surfaced in her mind. Gertie swallowed the lump of tears rising in her throat, and what bubbled back up was hot anger, rendering her throat raw. "You're lucky I've let you live this long."

"So what, you're going to kill me?"

"I'm not going to do anything. You are." Gertie pointed to the noose. "Kill yourself."

"What?"

"Kill yourself, you soulless fucking harpy."

Now it was Magic's turn to laugh.

"You can kill yourself now, or you can kill yourself in fifteen minutes. Your choice."

"Why would it—"

"Because all the women you ever preyed upon—everyone you manipulated and abused—have recorded videos and TikToks, which they will release en masse at that time. Actually, I think some of it has already leaked. Checked your Google reviews this morning and there are a few local guides calling you a narcissist. *Whomp-whomp.*"

"What?"

Gertie enunciated every word as she spoke. "In fifteen minutes, your empire will be over. You can choose to die now, or you can do it alone."

Magic's lips drew back in a snarl, revealing coffee-stained teeth. "Like I would ever give you the satisfaction of watching me die, you greasy bitch."

"Greasy or moisturized? Your skin doesn't seem to know the difference." Gertie sighed. "You could've made this easy on yourself. You could've returned the photo albums, said your last goodbyes, but no, you had to be a self-important little cunt about it."

Magic laughed. "If she knew who you really were—"

"And there's the problem, Magic. You always thought I was stupid." Magic gaped as Bea entered the room. She strode up behind Gertie, placing a hand on her shoulder. "I know who she is," Bea said. "But you keep changing for every girl you meet, like a chameleon. It didn't start with me, and it didn't end with me, but it can end today."

"You... Beatrice," Magic cried out, horrified. "You said you loved me. You—you used to love me."

Bea blinked. "I never said that."

"You *felt* it!"

"Noooo, I don't think I did."

"So—so you want me to *die*?"

Bea shrugged. "I mean, what's the confusion here?"

Faced with her reality, Magic's eyes watered with tears. She stamped her feet on the ground like a toddler, exaggerated screeches escaping her lips. Bea sighed and sat on Gertie's lap, and Gertie hugged her close, watching their caterwauling captive throw a temper tantrum.

"You live in the middle of nowhere," Gertie said. "Scream as much as you want, no one is coming for you. Security system's been shut down. You're only prolonging the inevitable."

"Fuck you!" she screamed. "And fuck you too, Bea! Where is my fucking dog?"

"Your dog is fine. I'm not a complete monster like you. I wouldn't let her die, but I might let her eat your corpse." Gertie shrugged. "Depends on how long it takes people to find you."

"I don't deserve to die because I—"

"But you do. You do. Because the thing is, Magic, you never loved Bea. If you *really* loved Bea, there's no way you would've left Westley alive." Gertie rubbed Bea's thigh, resting her head between her breasts.

Magic flinched, and she sucked in a deep breath of air through her mouth, chest heaving. The full horror of what Gertie admitted to was sinking in, and with it, hopelessness. Those blue eyes glazed over, turning an ashy white. Trembling and sobbing, she approached the chair, then climbed up on it. Perhaps she was deep in grief. Perhaps she thought that losing in such a humiliating way made escaping not worth it.

Whatever the reason, she put the noose on, and took the step off the chair.

As it clattered to the floor behind her, the rope pulled taut on the banister, and she kicked, coughing, sputtering for air. Her legs pumped ferociously and her fingers dug at the rope around her neck. Her eyes widened, revitalized, a summer sky devoid of clouds after a thunderstorm. Choked gasps and snarls escaped her pufferfish lips, and muscle tremors pulsated through her body.

She was regretting her decision.

With a trembling hand, she reached for them in a silent plea. Her legs kicked in the air desperately, and a cacophony of cracks—the bones and vertebrae of her neck splitting apart—echoed through the air. Bea's chest heaved, watching the scene unfold. For a moment Gertie worried she was having a panic attack, but then she noticed her half-lidded eyes and rosy cheeks.

"Don't tell me you're *horny*, Beatrice?"

Her blush deepened, and she leaned in close, lips pressed to her ear. "I mean... It's kinda hot, seeing you on a power trip."

Gertie's heart throbbed in her chest, and suddenly her mouth grew damp. She licked her lips, squeezing Bea's thighs again, eliciting a murmur of satisfaction. Gertie glanced at their victim, still struggling, then back at Bea. Something uncertain stirred within her stomach. Even for Bea—Bea, who hadn't even cried when Gertie admitted to killing her firstborn son—this seemed wild.

Bea's fingers looped small circles under the collar of her shirt. "Makes me almost wish I had been there when Westley..." She smiled. "Well...you know."

Oh she's not fucking around. "You want an audience for the next six minutes?"

"You think you can make me come in six minutes?"

"Oh Bea, I can make you come faster than that. She's just going to be alive for that long. This kind of hanging is slow, since we're not throwing her over a ledge." Looking up at Bea again, she spoke with a purr. "I don't want you to *suffer...*"

Bea winced, breathless. "I might be suffering."

"Show me."

Biting her lip, Bea guided Gertie's hand below the waistband of her jeans.

"You *were* suffering, you poor thing."

Bea shuddered and rolled her hips against Gertie's fingers, stifling a moan.

Gertie used her other hand to lift up Bea's shirt, pinching and twisting a pert nipple. "You want to make her watch, Bea? Want her to see how good I can make you come?"

Bea whimpered, nodding her head. Gertie gestured for her pants, then the rest of her clothes. Bea stood there naked, shivering, attempting to return to her arms, only for Gertie to make her face their dying captive.

"Patience, baby. I want her to see what she lost. Every glorious inch of you." She licked the center of Bea's back, tracing up her spine, as her fingers rubbed her clit. "Feels good?"

"M-more," Bea gasped. "I—I need more."

With a smile, Gertie gestured for Bea to take her seat. Bea glanced over at Magic, who was still struggling, her legs kicking. Her bloated tongue poked over her lips, and her face was completely red, but blue was seeping in, muddying her complexion. She had clawed so much at the noose her fingers were stained with blood. One of her fingernails was peeling off, the inflamed nail bed visible beneath. Piss flooded the front of her pants, dripping down her leg to mingle with the blood that had dripped onto the floor.

"Sit down. That's an order."

Blushing, Bea sat down, continuing to watch Magic struggle. Gertie removed her glasses, smirking as she crouched to her knees, careful not to injure herself. Hardwood floors were hell on her joints.

"You're a lucky girl," she whispered. "Two presents in one day."

She pressed her face against Bea's crotch, inhaling her scent, before diving in. Her cries of pleasure were interrupted by Magic's gasps and sputtering for air, but Bea was so far gone, they didn't register to her. One of her hands gripped the back of Gertie's head, and the other stretched underneath her shirt to play with her breasts.

Gertie pulled away to take a breath, eyes glazed over. She used a damp hand to brush her curls from her face. Was it just her imagination, or did Bea taste sweeter today? Bea whimpered as she writhed, begging for Gertie to fuck her, but she wouldn't give her what she wanted. Not yet.

"Who do you belong to?" Gertie growled as her fingers picked up the pace. "Tell that bitch."

"You," Bea gasped, her body convulsing like rolling thunder. "I belong to you."

"And is it better when I fuck you?"

"O-oh god yes..."

"Say it. Louder."

"You fuck me better," Bea cried, and she hissed, throwing back her head as she rolled her hips against Gertie's fingers. "Please, baby, *please!*"

"Good girl." With a chuckle, Gertie licked her lips and leaned in again.

Bea did not stop screaming until Magic had drawn her last breath.

Seventeen

THE CLEANUP WAS SIMPLE for Kayle and his crew. Dusting off some fingerprints, eliminating security footage, a handwritten suicide note—all of it perfectly planned.

"They're not going to be able to tell she died before the videos were posted, right?" Bea asked.

Kayle shook his head. "No. They can't determine an exact time. Fifteen minutes wouldn't make a difference. Trust me. Been doing this a long time."

Before long, Bea and Gertie were driving back to the private airport they landed at early that morning. Once Kayle and his crew completed the job, they would head home on a separate flight, which Gertie had already paid for.

In the back of the car, Bea looked at Gertie. "Could I see your phone?"

Gertie nodded and passed it to her. She watched Bea fumble through various apps, scanning through multiple hashtags. She chewed on her lip, and although her eyes watered, she didn't cry.

"Twelve women?" she whispered.

Gertie nodded.

"Jesus."

She stretched out her hand. "I don't think you should watch those, babe."

With a disappointed sigh, Bea returned the phone to Gertie. "Why do I never see the red flags in people?"

"Because you weren't taught to."

"I thought after Westley I would've learned."

Gertie shook her head. "You were vulnerable when you left Westley. Knowing how to spot the flags wouldn't have made a difference. It wasn't your fault."

Bea bit her lip again. She was clearly unconvinced, but nodded regardless.

Gertie reached into her purse and withdrew a manilla envelope. "Kayle found this in her office."

Bea opened it and withdrew the photos, spreading them across her lap. Her eyes watered. Countless cherub baby faces stared up at her. She sniffled, holding up one of River, sitting in a kiddie pool with a bucket on his head, a toothless smile spreading across his face.

"This is one of my favorites. Riv and his little floaties..." Bea hugged the folder to her chest. "Thank you, Gertie. Thank you."

"Of course. Um, I..." Gertie squeezed her eyes shut. "Stop me if this isn't the time to ask this question, but..."

"But..."

"Um... Is she *why* you don't want to be...intimate like that?"

Bea took a deep breath. She nodded, eyes staring at the ceiling as though trying to articulate what to say. After several moments, she spoke again. "She accused me of losing control. And when you got hurt, I thought...she was right." She blinked back tears. "It sounds stupid, but when you hit your head, I remembered when we were kids, and...the tile wall."

Gertie's eyes widened. *The tile wall.* When Bea assaulted her in their middle school bathroom, she had banged her head into the tile wall so hard she bled. The head wound she got from their sex accident wasn't nearly as bad, and was completely accidental, but it sent Bea back to the bathroom stall nonetheless. All these years, Gertie never imagined Bea could've been traumatized from something she perpetuated. Gertie had rejected her advances, which hurt her feelings, but thinking about what happened afterwards—their separation, the trauma of a police investigation and conviction for her uncle—no wonder Bea freaked out. Hurting Gertie, hurting *any* of her partners, resulted in nothing but horrible consequences for her, accident or not.

"I know you would *never* hurt me."

"But I already have. *Twice.*"

"I think you need to be gentle with yourself. I don't hold any guilt over the things I've done, and those were objectively worse. Not to mention, I fully had the intention of hurting you at one point, and you're not scared of me, right? So why should I be scared of you?"

"Well, the difference is that I actually deserved it." She crossed her arms, eyes focused on the floor.

"You don't honestly think I was in the right, do you?"

"Well, I don't know, Gertie. I knew how it felt to be assaulted, and I tried to do it to you, so..."

"We were children. Who taught kids about consent back then?"

"If it wasn't an acceptable excuse at the coffee shop, it's not now."

"Yes, but..." Gertie took a deep breath. "You didn't deserve to bear the brunt of that anger and have me fuck with your life. That was *me*, okay? That was me being prideful and not wanting to come to terms with the fact that you... You upended me."

"I know. I was trying to say... Hell, I don't know."

Seeing Bea was shutting down, she changed the subject. "We can talk more about this when you're ready. I'm sure you're tired."

"And you're not?" Bea smirked. "You were the one doing most of the work."

"*Cheeky.*" But Gertie smiled too.

With the fiasco they had so beautifully orchestrated, there was no need for anyone to suspect foul play in Magic's death. Kayle's team had done their job, and done it well. Once he got back to town, he came over to celebrate in the backyard with them, and to discuss payment details. The three of them clinked bottles of Mike's Hard together and toasted to their success. Similar to what Earl had done for Gertie in the past, Kayle suggested they think of a landscaping project to do in case they got audited, and they brought up the wedding.

Kayle rubbed his hands together, invigorated. "Ooh, I can work with that. Any flowers in mind?"

"Daisies," Bea said. "Those are our favorite."

Kayle smiled. "Yeah, I'm going to need more ideas than that. You've got a lot of space to fill."

Gertie and Bea exchanged a look, then shrugged.

"Uh, what about a color scheme?"

"I'm wearing a white dress, and she's wearing a black tux."

"No," Kayle said slowly, "a color scheme. Like, what color are the bridesmaids wearing?"

"Bridesmaids?" Bea wrinkled her nose. "Do we need those?"

"That sounds childish," Gertie agreed. "Do I need to stand up there with a gaggle of girlfriends, like some insecure college girl at a frat party?"

"Kellyanne would hate any dress you'd pick out for her, anyways."

"You are *so* right."

"Okay, okay." Kayle laughed, holding up his hands. "Ladies, I'm no wedding planner. But we're running out of time on some other business."

The women sighed, but gestured for him to continue. Kayle took another swig of his drink and ran his tongue over his teeth.

"Figured out he was getting released from prison in about two weeks. Now normally when a fella is released, he's either let outside the gates or has a bus take him into town. But per our tip from a guy on the inside, he's got a wife picking his ass up."

Bea frowned. "A wife? But he—he wasn't married."

"Outside of prison, no. But inside, he got married to a penpal. A Lorelai something or other. That ring a bell?"

Bea shook her head.

"Yeah. Figured it wouldn't, so I checked her out. She works at a thrift store in town. Inherited a house from her grandparents out in the woods. True crime fanatic, so that explains why she'd become a prisoner's pen pal to begin with. But it doesn't explain why she'd be his."

"Another sick fuck," Gertie said. "I don't think there's any great sense of mystery in that."

"Maybe you're right." Kayle looked between them. "So ladies, what do you want to do?"

Gertie glanced over at Bea, who was pale. She looked back at Kayle and silently motioned for him to give them a minute. He retreated to a corner of the yard and jammed a cigarette in his mouth, admiring the flowers. Gertie said nothing, but waited for her to speak.

"I think it's risky," Bea admitted, but she didn't outright say no.

"Do you want him dead?"

"Of *course* I do, but it's not about if I want him dead. Because more than wanting him dead, I want you to be by my side. And that? That takes priority over everything else." Bea sighed. "What we did with Magic, well... We'd be lucky if no one ties it back to us. But the thought of him wandering around in the world..."

"A restraining order…"

"Wouldn't work. Tried that with Westley. Didn't exactly stop him, did it?"

Gertie squeezed her hand. "Sweetheart, we can trust Kayle. No one will miss him but his gross little wife. If I kill him, he will never touch you *ever* again."

"I'm not worried about that." Bea's eyes welled with tears. "I'm worried about June. And River." She sobbed, her body trembling. "I'm worried he'll come for the kids."

"He won't. Because I'm going to skin him alive."

Eighteen

THE LOGISTICS WERE DIFFICULT to work out. Kayle watched Lorelai pick up Ernest from the prison, and followed them home. The plan was to stage a robbery gone wrong when Lorelai was out. They'd kill Ernest, and ransack the place. With it being so far on the outskirts of town, they didn't have much of a concern about the police showing up—not that they'd suspect the cops would care all that much.

After stalking them for a few days and determining Lorelai would *not* leave the house, Kayle rounded up a couple of his men and invaded in the dead of night. He then sent a car to pick up Bea and Gertie from their residence. As they pulled up to the house, they watched some of Kayle's men climb into their trucks. Gertie gave a friendly little wave and they responded in kind, as though they weren't about to murder a convicted pedophile.

Gertie helped Bea out of the car. "Do you want to wait outside? If you don't want to see him again, you don't have to."

Bea shook her head and squeezed her hand. "I'm with you now. I'm not afraid."

Hand in hand, the two approached the front steps of the ramshackle house. Peeling paint on the siding, patchwork roof, windows begging to be washed. Bird shit and tins of used chewing tobacco littered the front steps. The rancid smell was enough to make Gertie's eyes water, but she held her own, and proceeded inside the house.

Furniture pieces were overturned, walls smashed, valuables stashed in a to-go bag near the back door. In the center of the open-concept kitchen and living room, a man and a woman were tied to dining room chairs, their wrists and ankles bound behind them. Gertie noticed the woman first, who appeared young, perhaps younger than she was, though you wouldn't know that from her decrepit tobacco-yellow teeth. Ernest himself looked a little younger than expected, and bizarrely, the total opposite of Donald, Bea's father. Whereas Donald was so wrinkly and old that he resembled an ancient tree, Ernest was smooth-skinned like a mole rat, with beady eyes to match. Actually, the eyes were the only thing he visibly had in common with his brother.

Kayle beamed at Gertie with pride. "Welcome to the shindig."

"Is that what we're calling it?" Gertie smirked as she shrugged off her coat, making herself at home. Bea's coat remained on, and her arms wrapped around herself. "You okay?"

Bea nodded but didn't say anything. Gertie examined her captives closer. Lorelai's face was bruised, her nose a bloody pulp, lips smudged with blood. She sobbed and cowered in Gertie's gaze. But Ernest didn't. He sat straight up, one good eye twitching, staring intently. *Weird.* It took Gertie a minute, but she realized he was staring at her because he recognized her. Worms crawled and twisted within Gertie's stomach, spreading to the tips of every nerve in her body.

"No fucking way." Ernest swished the blood around in his mouth before spitting it on the ground.

"Pleasant," Gertie commented.

"I knew about the rumors, but didn't think it was true." Ernest stared past Gertie, looking at Bea. "Hey, princess. Don't you want to come see your Uncle Ernie?"

"Oh, no, none of that shit, you sick fuck." Gertie clocked him clear across the face, and Kayle hooted and hollered with delight.

"Let us go," Lorelai begged. "My husband served his time, he—"

Gertie smacked her as well. "Don't want to hear it."

Lorelai squealed in pain, spitting out a tooth, and bloody brown saliva. *Wow, performing free dental work. Add that to my list of charitable exploits.* Bea continued to hover at the back of the room, and Gertie paid her no mind. She wouldn't pressure her to get closer. The smell of rot coming from Lorelai's mouth alone was enough to make her want to puke.

"Why're you putting your hands on my wife?" Ernest snapped, blood dribbling down his lips. "I don't know why you're so fucking mad with me, lady! I didn't do nothing to you!"

"You can believe that if you want." Gertie looked at Kayle. "What've you got?"

"Pliers, a meat cleaver, a cattle prod—"

"Meat cleaver, please." It only seemed fitting to use one again. Kayle retrieved the item from the kitchen, then placed it in her hands. Even as Gertie's fingers closed around the handle, Ernest was unperturbed, instead continuing to chuckle, as though watching a comedy routine. Seriously? She had smacked the shit out of his wife, and he still didn't consider her a threat? His eyes were now on Bea, and Gertie loathed the way he looked at her. She tried to block his view, but he wriggled and twisted his head to keep her in his sight.

"What," Ernest said, "did you hang around her house long enough that she finally invited you in?"

Green bloomed across Bea's face. Gertie looked between her and Ernest, confused, unsure of what to say. Bea exited the shack, calm and collected, like leaving a school building during a fire drill. Grimacing, Gertie passed the weapon to Kayle. Lorelai moaned in agony, begging for mercy in her nasally voice.

"Good work here—I gotta go after her. In the meantime, go nuts."

"Ma'am?" Kayle asked, his voice cracking with surprise.

"You've earned it, Kayle. You get the first stab at him." Gertie winked. "Just save some for me, okay?"

"M-ma'am—thank you, ma'am. I've got it covered."

"I know you do." And with that, she took off after Bea.

"Beatrice!"

Her fiancée stalked along the pathway, shoulders bunched up like she was cold—which she could've been, it was an oddly chilly day for an Ohioan summer. Gertie huffed and puffed, her boots grappling for balance against the sudden steep inclines. She wondered if these were trails actually meant for hikers, or if they were for those goddamn Tony Hawk wannabe mountain bikers. Her heel almost crunched under her as she took another drop, threatening send her tumbling down the hill.

"Bea!"

Finally, Bea stopped and turned to face her. The nausea had receded from her complexion, and instead her cheeks were cherry red; angry. "Why can't you give me space?"

"Because you're upset?"

"I'm upset because I didn't want to do this," Bea retorted, voice hoarse.

Gertie blinked, confused. "But you told me you did."

"Would you have listened to me if I didn't?"

"Bea, you said you were worried about the kids."

"Yeah, well—"

"This isn't about us committing murder, this is about you being upset about what he said. Why can't we talk about it? Whatever it is, I'm sure it's not that bad."

Bea didn't say anything. Kicked at a rock with the toe of her boot.

Anger stirred in Gertie's voice. "Why can't you talk to me?"

"Because I don't want to."

Gertie swallowed a lump in her throat. The coldness in Bea's voice prickled the goosebumps on her arms. "You can't build walls when I'm trying to build bridges. That's not fair. You always do this when I try to comfort you."

Bea mumbled, "I don't know what you're talking about."

"Really? Let's rewind." Gertie ticked off the incidents on her fingers. "Your parents died, you didn't want me to touch you. Magic sent you those photos, you didn't want me to touch you. When news about your uncle got out, you didn't want me to touch you, and tried to tell me to go to work when you *were sick and bedridden and clearly needed my help*. And now we're doing it again. I shouldn't have to beg you to let me in, Bea. If you don't trust me to comfort you when things are hard, why are we getting married?"

"Well, we don't have to get married."

From the way she was averting her eyes, she clearly knew it was a ludicrous, childish thing to say. Gertie waited in patient silence, hoping she would take it back.

But she didn't.

"Why are you doing this to me?" Gertie whispered. "I *know* you don't mean it. I know you're hurting. I just want to help."

Bea spread her hands helplessly, voice steeped in aggravation. "Every time you help, you make it worse! We're killing two, possibly three, more people? It's—it's too much!"

"You're right! I can't take the stress, and I don't like what this is doing to us. But if we finish the job, no one will fuck with us ever again. And I can't let him walk away, knowing what he's done to you. I'm sorry, but I can't."

Bea rubbed her face. "I know. And I won't fight you on that. I just can't be a part of it."

"T-that's fine. Do you want to go home? I can have a car take you—"

"For Chrissakes, Gertrude." Her voice dropped to a whisper, her eyes squeezing shut. "I need you to leave me alone."

Flabbergasted, Gertie watched as Bea disappeared into the thicket. Choking back a sob, Gertie pressed her hands over her nose and mouth, suppressing a small scream of frustration. *This isn't her. This isn't who she is.* Bea was not vindictive, unkind, or uncommunicative. Bea was her sunshine. Her carpool karaoke partner. Her best friend. The one who dried her tears when she cried about Jack, who made her delicious fancy lunches, who practiced cheer moves with their daughter in the backyard. For as much as this hurt, Bea was not a culmination of her worst moments.

And Gertie remembered that the man who had put Bea through quite a few of them was wrapped up like a Christmas tree gift, awaiting his grisly fate. The thought dried her tears instantly.

Nineteen

WHEN GERTIE RETURNED TO the shack, she found Ernest had eight more stab wounds than before, along with two vertical slices along his ears, and an odd bloody puddle soaking through the crotch of his denim jeans. Sweat and blood coagulated on his face in messy, goopy rivers that obscured his vision. Viscous vomit bubbled from between his lips, dripping onto the floor. Lorelai—thank Christ—had duct tape over her wretched mouth now, so although she wailed, it wasn't as annoying as before.

Kayle's chest heaved as he stood over Ernest, eyes dilated, knife in hand. He gulped down a breath, the adrenaline in his eyes dissipating the closer Gertie got.

"Might've gotten carried away."

"You stabbed me in the dick," Ernest rasped, writhing in his seat. "The fuck do you mean?"

Gertie patted Kayle on the back. "Meat cleaver?"

"Right here." He grabbed it off the fireplace mantle and passed it to her.

Weapon in hand, Gertie walked over to the kitchen area, grabbed another chair, and raked it across the floorboards, scraping them up as much as she could. Lorelai whimpered as Gertie set the chair in front of Ernest, and she plopped in her seat with a satisfied grunt.

"Alright, motherfucker. You had fun running your mouth, right?" Gertie asked. "Did you want to provide context for that shitty thing you said, or no?"

Ernest gritted his teeth in an attempted smile. "I can't believe you don't know."

"You're boring me, Ernest. You really are." She ran her finger along the dull edge of the meat cleaver. It was a curved blade, different from the one she had at home. Either it would be more difficult to use, or more fun—her nerves prickled with excitement. "When Bea told me stories, I pictured someone more menacing, but it feels right that you're this pathetic."

Ernest seemed confused by that statement. Gertie checked the sharp side of the cleaver, pricking her finger against it. She grimaced at the bead of blood that bubbled from the minuscule cut. Kayle offered her a page of sandpaper, which she quickly used to sharpen it. Horror surfaced in Ernest's eyes as he watched her work.

"I've done this before," Gertie told him, smiling. "You didn't know that? You should've heard the way your brother screamed. He begged me to spare him. God, it was—*delicious.*"

"He died in a car wreck, you fucking bitch."

"Oh Ernest, *really?* You really thought the car conveniently exploded?"

Gertie cackled, and Kayle chuckled too. Amused, she watched as the color drained from his face. Lorelai sobbed. She sounded like a dolly from the Isle of Misfit toys. With one sharp-eyed glare, Gertie silenced her.

"Hey," Ernest said. "I get it. You're a mother. What mother wouldn't want to kill someone like me?"

"Listen to him," Kayle said. "He won't even admit what he's done."

"Whatever," Ernest spat. "Bea walked away from you, lady. You've got nothing to do with this. She ain't worth the fucking trouble, that's for sure. I got years in the slammer proving that point."

Gertie stared at him. "Not worth the trouble?"

Ernest bit his tongue. It seemed like he knew he had fucked up, especially when Gertie started to play with the cleaver again.

"Bea is—was—so perfect. More charismatic than any pageant queen, a great sense of humor, undeniably gorgeous... You worked so hard to whittle away at her, and now you think she's not worth it. Typical." Gertie paused. "I'm sure you know that something happened between her and me back then. Something that led to you rotting away in a cell for a long, long time."

"I know what happened."

"Then you know you didn't just hurt her. You hurt me, too. You hurt me through the actions you taught her. You hurt me because things might've turned out differently between us. You hurt me because I'm in love with a woman who cries herself to sleep at night over the things you did to her. So make no fucking mistake, this is personal any way you roll the dice."

"Why're you defending her?" He barked, blood frothing in his mouth. "That little bitch has always had a psychotic streak. And she's always been obsessed with you. She used to pretend it was you when—"

Gertie cracked her fist against his cheek, snapping his head to the side. Lorelai sobbed, and even though it was muffled by the tape, Gertie couldn't stand the sound of her voice any longer. "Get her out of here, Kayle."

Lorelai screamed and wrestled as Kayle dragged her from the room. Gertie reached for the roll of duct tape on the table beside Ernest, who was wriggling against his restraints. Excitement bubbled within her chest, and her heartbeat echoed in her ears like a drum. She stuck the duct tape to his forehead and began to circle him, wrapping the long strand around his head as though it were the center of a ball of yarn, crossing over his mouth, his cheeks, his nose.

Kayle returned to the room. "What are you doing, ma'am?"

"You're going to stand this fucker up in a second. But I don't want him to head butt you." She crossed the tape over his nose again, providing thick padding. His entire head was now engulfed in tape, leaving only his eyes and ears exposed. Gertie stared at him, snapping the last of the strip off the spool. The man hyperventilated, unable to breathe. His chest heaved in desperation, and his body fought against his restraints. "If you haven't figured it out by now, this is more about me than it ever was about her. In all honesty, she was against it. And this woman you insist is worthless—is so kind and loving, that she's letting me do this, because she knows how important it is to me.

"So take it in, Ernest. I'm the last thing you're ever going to see. And I want you to know that as I'm delighting in ending your life in the most painful way possible, I'm doing it *because* she's worth it." She leaned in close. "Say hi to your brother for me in hell."

She wrapped the tape over his eyes, and Ernest's muffled screams struggled to break through their sticky barrier. Gertie laughed. She slashed the restraints that bound his ankles and wrists. In one swift motion, Kayle forced him to his feet. Gertie picked up Kayle's knife and cut away the clothing he wore, leaving him in his dripping, bloody underwear. Discordant sobs echoed beneath the duct tape mask, but Gertie felt no pity for him. She imagined the times Bea had been humiliated like this by him, and she moved more aggressively. As the knife sliced through the cloth, it nicked into his skin, separating skin and muscle. He reared back, trying to get away, but Kayle's grip was stronger. With an eager grin, Kayle jammed his fingers into the oozing lacerations, twisting them. It was as though Ernest had become a meat puppet, easy to manipulate.

"Clever," Gertie said to him.

In response, Kayle beamed.

Grabbing her machete again, Gertie took a deep breath. Then she threw the cleaver into his backside, right where the top of his ass connected with his spine in a perfect symmetrical line. He crumpled, bone bursting through the flesh like a blackhead popping out of a freshly burst zit, somehow gooier than expected. Blood frothed from the gash, and Ernest spasmed, choking and screaming, legs wobbling underneath his weight. Gertie peeled the cleaver from the spot, admiring the depth of the first strike. Kayle held him upright as Gertie hacked again, continuing to work her way up his back, blood and blubber spraying from the gushing wounds. Fraying skin peeled away from the spine like torn wrapping paper. Muscle ripped apart, sinew by sinew, scraps fluttering to the ground like confetti; spattering Gertie in the face. He howled and screamed and writhed, but Gertie didn't relent.

In fact, it only made her hit him that much harder—to the point where, well, she accidentally hit a little too deep. Her machete lodged within his ribcage, splintering one of his lungs, causing a geyser of blood to explode in her face. With her free hand she reached in to clear away the chunks of bone she had shattered, throwing them to the floor. As she struck again, she delighted in the resistance of the machete handle, the way his parched body slurped the weapon further in, organs and blood clamoring to fill the damaged space. Each new organ that she saw—kidney, intestine, liver—she carved a chunk from. He choked and coughed up blood, so much that despite the thickness of the mask, it bubbled through crevices in the tape strips, rolling down his chin, dripping onto the floor. It was at that moment Kayle finally dropped him, disgusted. Together the two hovered over the dying man. Urine soaked the floor, mingling with the blood and globs of flesh they had ripped from his body. Somehow, amid his coughing, Ernest managed to plead for death.

Gertie crouched low beside him. "I'm not going to do that, Ernest. That's letting you off easy. You've had a lifetime of that. No..."

Gertie lobbed off two of his fingers, but he was so weak he couldn't conjure even a whimper of pain. She kicked aside the bloody digits, watching them roll across the floor, before lifting up her cleaver and hammering it down on the rest, crunching them beneath the dulling blade.

"You made her bleed countless times over. So I'm going to drain you dry."

It was a fraction of what he deserved.

Twenty

ONCE ERNEST WAS DEAD, Kayle assured her he'd take care of cleaning up the body. When asked what to do with Lorelai, Gertie shrugged her shoulders, walked outside, and cried into her hands. She waited on the rancid porch steps for a good hour, waiting for Bea to return, but she didn't.

"Get some rest, ma'am," Kayle said. "I'll keep watch for her, and we'll figure out what to do with the lady-creep in the morning. I'll have one of the guys take you home."

Reluctantly, Gertie agreed, but only because she was exhausted. She went home, scrubbed herself raw in the shower, and crawled into bed, dead to the world. No more than an hour later, she awoke to the sound of Bea stumbling through the door. Gertie sat up, squinting in the faint light. A silver strip of moonlight split the room down the center, half of Bea's face visible in its shine. Even through bleary eyes, she could see that Bea had been crying.

"Do you hate me?"

Drowsy, Gertie shook her head. She held open her arms, and Bea fell into them, sobbing. Gertie rubbed circles against her back, trying to calm her down. Bea straddled her lap, her face buried against her shoulder; tears dampening her nightgown.

"Where have you been? You feel like an iceberg."

Bea sniffled. "I went for a walk. Had to clear my head."

Nodding, Gertie helped unzip her jacket. "Change and you can warm up under the covers with me, okay?"

"Why're you being so nice to me?" Bea whispered, tears rolling down her cheeks. "I was awful to you."

"Because I know you don't mean it."

"I don't deserve that."

"Yes, you do." Gertie wiped away her tears. "And I'll keep telling you that until you believe it."

"But—why?" Bea warbled. "I'm so selfish. I pushed you away and you didn't deserve it. I'm sorry. I'm so, so sorry."

Gertie soothed her, continuing with the small circles. "You have every right to be mad at me. Our fight made me realize that I strongarmed you into the murders, and that was wrong. You're my partner, and you should feel like you have equal say in things."

"You didn't make me feel any type of way." Bea wiped her eyes. "I don't care about you killing people. I care about you getting *caught* from killing people. I love—I love seeing you in your element, whether it's giving a speech behind a podium or with a cleaver in hand. But actions have consequences, and... I want to protect you too, you know?"

"I know. And I'm sorry I bulldozed you. And about the touching thing... I know I'm not entitled to touch you. It's just... It's like when you do that without telling me you don't *want* to be touched, it makes me feel like I'm part of the problem. Like I'm the thing that hurt you." Gertie laughed, blinking back tears. "But I guess I've done that already."

"No, Gertie. No." Bea cupped her face in her hands. "It's me. I'm the mess. I—I shouldn't shut down. I should tell you what I need, even if that means asking you for space."

"We can work on it. It'll be okay."

Bea exhaled. "There's something else. I… I know I haven't been honest with you about so many things as of late, but you deserve to know the truth."

"Sure. You can tell me."

She took a deep breath. So much love, so much fire, in those silver eyes. She stood up and paced the floor for several moments before gathering the courage to speak again. "From the minute I walked through the door to Ms. Weisel's classroom in the third grade, you were it. You were my girl. But you—you didn't know it yet."

"I don't understand."

Bea squeezed her eyes shut. "I've been stalking you. Almost our whole lives."

The wind rushed from Gertie's chest. "*What?*"

"You never thought it was weird when I followed you to the bathroom, over and over again?"

"No, I… Well, I mean, I didn't think you were *stalking* me, so much as it was easy to find out where I was at. We were in the same school, for Chrissakes. What do you mean by stalking? You mean stuff happened outside of school?"

Bea nodded, squeezing her eyes shut. "Um, in the fourth grade, I figured out where you lived and I used to walk my dog by it. In middle school, even after that whole fiasco, I'd ride my bike there and watch you from the hill behind it for hours. You never closed your curtains back then." Bea twiddled her thumbs. "My plan was whenever I figured my shit out and worked up the courage to tell you how I felt that I'd... I'd know your routine by heart, and I could... I don't know, come up with some way to worm myself into your life? Either that, or find a way to blackmail you into being with me. I'll admit I'm not exactly a criminal mastermind."

"But you never went through with it."

"Well, no, because you and Jack started dating. So then the plan became, well, I'll wait for him to dump you, swoop in, be the knight in shining armor. But he didn't. He loved you. Because *of course* he loved you. And when it became clear I wasn't—I wasn't going to have my chance, my jealousy got worse. I followed you on dates with him... There was a movie night you guys had a flat tire. That was me. Um... I'd take tissues or things you had used off of tables at restaurants you'd been to, and one time you left behind a lipstick—"

Gertie's jaw dropped. "My Magenta Maude lipstick?!"

Bea winced. "Maybe?"

"Goddamn it, I *loved* that shade. What happened to it?"

"Nefarious things."

"Oh good god."

"My parents got worse, so I gave up physically stalking you at the end of high school, because my number one priority became leaving their house. But even when I was with Westley—I mean, I never stopped thinking about you. And by that time we had social media. It was so easy to make a random profile and look at your pages, and..."

Gertie frowned. "So you knew when we met in the Wus' restaurant that I was a widow and had a daughter?"

"Yes," Bea whispered. "I knew, and I played dumb. I wanted you to like me. I wanted to start over. I wanted you to believe I had changed. And we all know how that worked out."

Gertie bit her lip. "Okay. Um... So did you know I was going to the restaurant?"

"No, that was by chance." Bea blushed at the memory. "God, if I *had* planned on that, I wouldn't have let you pay for my meal. That was so embarrassing."

"What about the daisies?"

"The...daisies?"

"In the bouquet you gave me on our first date. You gave me five daisies, just like Jack did for me when we were kids. Did you know about the daisies?"

"I forgot about that story. No. I wish I was that smart, but no."

"Alright then." Gertie pinched the bridge of her nose, trying to process it all. "Is there anything else I should know about?"

She winced. "Yeah. Um, remember when we put up our Christmas tree? And we had that amazing night together?"

"Y-yes." Back then, Bea had been so lustful, so excited. She had unveiled an early lingerie present for the two of them to enjoy—and enjoy it they did, and some nights thereafter since.

"Well, I knew about Westley way longer than I let on. I had the security app on my phone pretty much the weekend after I moved in. I got the notification that a person was at our front door, and I watched as you took out the body parts and the furniture pieces with Earl, and *god*, thinking you had killed him for me? I was soaking wet the entire drive home. Back then I thought you killing him meant that—that you were in love with me, and I...wanted to celebrate."

"Oh, Beatrice," Gertie whispered. "I'm so sorry. That must have hurt your feelings."

"Why are *you* apologizing? I'm the one who acted like a crazy person."

"If you're crazy, what does that make me?" Gertie smirked, but Bea did not lighten up.

"I don't know. All I know is that lying to you for so long is a violation of your trust."

"So was me killing your parents and son. Why're you so upset about this?"

"Because I'm ashamed. When you fell in love with me, you saw me the way I've always *wanted* you to see me. A-as soft and delicate and gentle. As someone who loves you, who stands by you, who would do *anything* for you. It's why you don't believe me when I tell you I'm worried about hurting you. You don't know how gross and awful I've always been.

"And then I think: shit. Maybe I bring out the worst in you. You started murdering people after you met me. Like yeah, you've always had homicidal urges or violent thoughts, but *I* was the catalyst." Her voice quaked, and she wiped at her eyes. "I feel like I'm this sickness that's infected your life, and sometimes I have to wonder... I have to wonder if I deserve you, and if I make your life better." She sobbed. "I mean, look at me. We have everything I've ever wanted for us, and I can't even be happy about it, because I know I'm going to ruin it."

That admission was a gut punch. Gertie had to gulp down air to make sure she didn't buckle under the weight of her words. Part of her wanted to collapse into herself, to become a black hole that the universe would swallow and pull to shreds, but even in this moment she knew this wasn't about her.

This was about Bea.

And this wasn't the first time they had a conversation about this sort of thing—she remembered the day after the press got wind of Ernest, how Bea said she didn't feel good enough for her. Gertie thought she had convinced her otherwise, but it had taken her until this moment to realize Bea was always going to need reassurance. She would always question her self-worth. She would always enter rooms on eggshells. She would always be clingy, jealous, and neurotic.

But Gertie was all of those things too. And selfish and shameful as it was, she loved that about Bea. She loved the constant *craving* that Bea had for her; loved being the center of her universe. She reveled in the satisfaction that came with providing for her and hearing her insist she was spoiled. She'd bask in the glow of Bea's warm gaze and listen to the sweet melody of her praises until the day she died.

In the end, what separated love from reciprocal worship?

She reached out, gently taking her hands, kissing her knuckles. "Bea, I *still* think you're soft and delicate. If the BDSM and kink stuff didn't change that, why would this? You just—you love *so* hard, angel. You have all these big, beautiful feelings, and that's one of my favorite things about you. I don't feel things like you do. Before I met you, I was...numb to everything but anger." Gertie blinked back tears. "I was like a passenger in a driverless car. I had power for the sake of having power, but I wasn't—I wasn't living up to my full potential. And you, in part, helped me realize it. You showed me how wonderful life could be. You think I could've gotten this far without your help? You take care of the house, our meals, *and* the kids. Does that sound like a sickness to you?"

Bea bit her lip. "No... But you would've found a way. You're the one who knows how to get things done. At the end of the day, all I know is violence and sex."

"*Beatrice.* That is *so* not true. You know how to make kale taste delicious, how to draw little Post-It note comics for my lunches—"

"That's all pointless—"

"—how to make our kids smile when they're sad. How to kiss me until I forget how to breathe. How to light up a room." Gertie's voice ran hoarse. "None of that is pointless."

Bea's reply was hollow. "Someone else could learn how to do all those things."

"No, Bea. They're not you." She ran her fingers through her hair. "You know, I used to think I was so gross no one would ever love me. But Jack came along and showed me differently. And I'm so, so sorry that I haven't done the same."

"It's not your fault."

"It is. You told me you accepted every part of me, but you don't know I'd do the same for you." Gertie fixed her gaze upon her, her brown eyes warm yet piercing, holding Bea to her place. "Loving you has never been a burden. No matter how many people I've skinned and slaughtered, nothing was ever too much. If I had to start over at that Chinese restaurant, the only thing I'd do differently is love you right from the start."

Bea's eyes welled with tears, and she sucked in a breath as though she had been slapped. "Oh." Her body seized in a sob, folding in on itself. "*Oh.*" Gertie pulled her back into her lap, into her arms, into where she belonged.

"Y-you're—you're sure?"

"I mean, the knife play was an adjustment! But never too much, no."

"And you're not afraid of me?"

"No, baby. I know exactly how 'disgusting' you are, and I wouldn't have you any other way."

Gertie reached for a tissue from the nightstand, and helped Bea dry her tears.

"I didn't mean it when I said I didn't want to marry you. You know that, right?"

"I know. Like I said, big feelings."

Bea sighed. "From now on, I'll try not to throw tantrums when I'm upset."

Gertie laughed, pressing her face against her chest. She smelled like sweat and pine and cedar. She wanted nothing more than to breathe her in.

"I can't believe you're not mad."

"I mean, I *am* mad. Stealing my favorite lipstick? How'd that even do anything for you?"

Delighted, Gertie watched as Bea gulped a nervous lump down her throat. As Bea parsed for her reply, she noticed how her chest heaved, how her fingers nervously played with the collar of her shirt.

"I-It's not hard to imagine, is it?"

"Unfortunately, I don't have that big of an imagination. I think you need to show me. Think of it as your punishment." Gertie snapped her fingers. "Drop those pants."

Biting her lip, Bea obeyed, standing up so she could wriggle them down. Gertie retrieved her tube of lipstick from her purse. She looked back at Bea.

"Everything off."

Twenty-One

GERTIE WOKE UP TO find Bea squeezing her like a boa constrictor. Drowsy silver eyes admired her, a soft smile on her lips. Gertie nestled closer to her warmth.

"What're you doing?"

Bea smiled. "Just looking at you, in the beautiful light of the morning sun."

"Aww, cornball." Gertie chuckled as Bea kissed her head.

"I wanted to ask you something... I, um, never..." She blinked hard. "I never got...*help* for what happened. I was court-ordered to go to a psychiatrist for a bit when I was a kid, but once I didn't have to go anymore, I... Well, I stopped. And um, I was thinking that before we get married, I want to make sure I'm in a better headspace. And, y'know, be a better communicator. I think part of the reason why I act the way I do is—like, a safety thing?"

Gertie nodded. For her it was easy to understand. Bea had never had relationships where she felt safe confiding in another person and expressing her emotions with them. Subconsciously, maybe Bea shut down because she was trying to avoid escalating conflict, or feel unsafe.

"But I know therapy can be expensive, since I don't have insurance right now, so…"

"Pfft, I can pay for that."

"You sure?"

"Yes. I'm proud of you. This is a big step!" Gertie squeezed her hand. "But I want you to do it for *you,* too. Not for me, or for the kids. Like I told you, you get to do things for yourself."

Bea smiled. "Thanks."

"Of course." Gertie frowned. "Do you know what time it is?"

Bea reached for her phone at the same time Gertie reached for hers. 8 a.m., but no messages from Kayle. Gertie frowned. Odd. He was a good communicator, and although they hadn't worked together long, he'd always give her updates on when he was working on something, or had finished a job.

For some reason, she felt an instinct to call him, but it rolled straight to voicemail. Frowning, she spoke with a few others she knew from Rose Landscaping on the encrypted messaging app Kayle had set up for her, but they also hadn't heard from him. One guy, Rocco, volunteered to go to the house to check on him, and report back. Gertie prepared coffee while Bea flipped omelets. Thirty-some minutes after she had spoken with Rocco, he called her.

"Shit went south."

He's just an employee. Gertie thought as she turned the key in the ignition of her truck. *Getting hurt on the job is to be expected.*

Still, she drove to see him.

Rocco had found Kayle in the house with four stab wounds in the abdomen, and Lorelai was nowhere to be seen. Rose Landscaping employed a doctor that worked under the table, so Kayle ended up at his hideaway. It was a ramshackle ranch house close to the train tracks, and as Gertie and Bea entered, the roar of the passing train's engine rattled the floor beneath them.

The doctor was a nondescript man no older than 65, bad teeth, but good skin. Reminded her of the dad from *Psych,* not that she could remember the name. June would know, though. He led her into Kayle's room, which had paint peeling off the walls. IV tubes crisscrossed his body like unkempt vines.

"Hi ma'am," Kayle said, coughing.

"Call me Gertie, for fuck's sake."

"Sure, ma—Gertie." He yawned, his hand moving to his injured abdomen. A conflicted expression crossed his face as he looked at her. With a heavy sigh, she came and sat down across from him, Bea standing behind her.

"What happened?"

"Bitch wriggled out of her bind. I feel goddamn stupid about it. I don't know how she did it."

"Did you see the fingernails on her?" Bea shuddered. "I wouldn't be surprised if she cut her way through the goddamn rope."

"Shit. Maybe she did." Kayle grunted. "Give me a day, and I'll go out looking for her."

Gertie scoffed. "Who, Lorelai? Fuck that. And you need more than a day to rest up."

She reached for the washbasin beside the bed, full of warm water. Suds sparkled across the surface. She dipped a washcloth into it, wrung it out, and wiped away some of the sweat on his forehead.

His cheeks flushed. "You can take the doc's bill out of my pay."

"*Puhlease.* Good employers should provide healthcare. Don't sweat it." She made another pass. "We'll wait for Lorelai to make her move, and deal with it then. We've got enough of a messy cleanup to deal with when it comes to Ernest."

"Okay." Kayle crumpled, eyes welling with tears. Gertie squeezed his hand, and he squeezed it back. "I-I thought this would..."

"Make you feel better?"

Kayle nodded, gulping down a sob.

Gertie sighed. "Sometimes vengeance doesn't feel the way it's supposed to. It's this burst of adrenaline, big and bright like fireworks, and when it fizzles out it...leaves you feeling empty like a starless sky."

"You feel it too, then?" Kayle sniffled. "I feel so stupid. It's over. I should be happy."

"The reason why you're not," Gertie said gently, "is because the damage was still done. The person you loved was still hurt. And in your case your person...isn't with us anymore. For that, Kayle, I am so sorry."

He continued to cry. Blinking back her own share of tears, Gertie embraced him tightly, careful to avoid his wounds. At this moment Kayle was not a grown man.

He was a teenage boy who missed his little brother.

Twenty-Two

UNFORTUNATELY FOR LORELAI, HER little disappearance made her the perfect scapegoat for Ernest's death. Kayle's crew restructured the disaster area to make it look like a domestic dispute. Carefully doctored notes, IOUs addressed to Ernest from unscrupulous sources, and a diary full of entries chronicled the dissolution of their marriage, well before he'd actually been released from prison. When the news splashed on the front page, a warrant was issued for her arrest, and she was officially on the run from the law.

Served the bitch right.

With Lorelai out of the picture, Gertie and Bea remained vigilant, but not too concerned. The closer she came to them, the more she'd risk, and she didn't have nearly enough resources to take them out. When she had escaped the house, she hadn't bothered to steal a car, so as far as they knew, she'd been running around like a stray dog. Still, they heightened security measures around their home and Gertie's office, and with Kayle coming over regularly to prep the backyard for the wedding, it'd be hard for her to catch them off guard. Kayle also offered to work security for the event, which assured them further peace of mind. They set the date for some time in July, after June's graduation party.

Over the course of the next year, they had more to busy themselves with. Bea started therapy, Gertie expanded her political empire under Zoya's tutelage, and the two prepared June for college, celebrating all the milestones that came with her senior year. Kayle and his crew spent day after day working on the garden, and Bea often invited the crew to eat dinner with them afterwards, making the house livelier than ever. It was funny to Gertie—when she was younger, her and Jack had imagined having a lively home with children, hosting boisterous family parties and entertaining guests throughout all the seasons. She never imagined that years after his death, she'd have that family now, Kayle and crew included.

Despite their ever-growing excitement for their union, planning remained tedious. Between the two of them, they couldn't make any solid decisions on what they wanted the wedding to look like, sans a few things, like daisies. Color schemes were a scientific equation they couldn't calculate and forget making choices on food. Two foodies such as them could *never* make a solid decision on what to eat, since they liked everything. At times, they both entertained the idea of a simple courthouse wedding, but knew that someone, potentially a huge supporter of Gertie, would feel snubbed. Gertie's strength as a politician remained in that she was connected to her community, and on the surface, extroverted; wanting to share as much of her life with others as possible. So, the courthouse wedding was out, but the wedding planner, Martha, was in.

Although Gertie and Bea had hired her, June had taken some aspects of the event upon herself. On the things they couldn't decide, June or Martha intervened to provide assistance. June even had a little color-coded planner that she carried with her, along with a pack of highlighters, and honestly, Gertie was beginning to question whether June had spent more time on her ACTs or this.

"Moms!" June said, traipsing into the living room one night after dinner, when they were trying to watch a show. Gertie resisted the urge to giggle when she saw Bea flinch and pause it. The endless barrage of questions had become exhausting. "Your rehearsal dinner is next week, and Martha wanted me to ask you, Mommy, who's walking you down the aisle?"

Gertie blinked. "I need someone to walk me down the aisle?"

"Wouldn't I walk her down the aisle?" Bea asked.

"We could do it like that," June said. "But then I'm going to have to tell the photographer you don't want reaction shots. Like, photos of you reacting to Mom when she comes down the aisle. You haven't seen her dress yet, so I think that'd be a missed opportunity."

"Oh." Bea blushed, looking over at Gertie. "I'd love to have those, actually."

Gertie smiled. "Then we'll have them."

"I figured you would. Besides, it's bad luck to see the bride in her dress before the altar. So, who is walking you down the aisle?"

Gertie sighed, rubbing her eyes. Traditionally speaking, her father would do it, but she hadn't spoken to him since she had married Jack. He had always scorned her for making such a hasty decision when she was so young, but in all honesty, she figured she'd made it easier for him when he decided to remarry and start a new family. She'd ask Jack's parents, but while they were happy for her, they were unable to attend the wedding. As consolation, they sent them a fine bottle of champagne.

"I don't know," Gertie admitted, quiet.

"Oh, well, I have like, the cutest idea. Since I'm your maid of honor, I thought I could walk *you* down the aisle and give you away, and then River can walk Bea down the aisle." June launched into an excited over explanation of how the wedding procession would go, acting out everything with her arsenal of highlighters.

"I think that's a wonderful idea, June."

"Hell yeah," Bea said. "Let's do it."

June squealed with delight, hugging her mothers, before whipping out her phone to call Martha. They listened to her jabber as she drifted out of the room, unable to breathe a sigh of relief until they heard her bedroom door close upstairs. Bea squeezed Gertie's hand, but didn't unpause the show.

"How're you feeling?" Gertie asked.

Bea smiled. "Excited. Maybe a little nervous, because there's so much that needs to go right, and so many ways that things can go wrong..."

"That DJ is iffy."

"Oh, for sure. I wouldn't expect a DJ to be anything else." Bea chuckled. "But yeah. I'm feeling good. Really excited to be Mrs. Beatrice Burns. I can't wait to see you walk down that aisle in your dress."

Gertie smiled. "And I can't wait to see you cry over it."

"*Pssh.*"

"Oh my god, why deny it? You're totally going to cry."

"I don't think I'm going to cry when you walk down the aisle, but I *will* cry when we're reading our vows. I will place a bet on that."

"Ooh, a bet?" Gertie teased. "With money, or your body?"

"*Gertrude.* You know I don't have money. And either way, I'm going to win."

One week and a rehearsal dinner later, and the big day had finally arrived. After a brunch filled with too many mimosas, Gertie was whisked off to the bedroom for hair and makeup. One by one, the other bridesmaids arrived, including Kellyanne, Joanna, Winnie, Laura, and Zoya. June multitasked between getting ready and assisting Martha with last minute touch-ups and details. Each of the bridesmaids were kind enough to bring Gertie drinks to sip on as she anxiously awaited the start of the wedding. For some reason, although she was only two doors down, she missed Bea terribly.

In the afternoon, she finally finished hair and makeup, and her bridesmaids helped her into her dress: a gorgeous ivory mermaid gown with off-the-shoulder sleeves—she figured she'd tease Bea at the altar while she could. June broke out a giant roll of boob tape, and together, the bridesmaids took their turns wrapping it around her. The more they worked, the more they sweated, and at a certain point, towels were passed around the room in a desperate attempt to clean themselves off. Once she was finally strapped in—the tape molded around her breasts and waists like a corset—she slipped into her dress.

June's gasp filled her ears. "*Mommy.*"

The sniffling bridesmaids fanned their faces and admired her in the mirror, and Gertie stared back at herself, stunned. She had loved the dress when she tried it on at the boutique, but to see it on her now... She couldn't believe she was the same person. Her black hair was wrapped into a bun on top of her head, a few stray curls framing her face. She admired herself in the mirror, turning from side to side.

At that moment, the instrumental version of Kehlani's *Honey* began to play outside. The bridesmaids ushered themselves out, trying to get to their places. Gertie watched through the window as the guests settled into their seats.

June wrapped an arm around her mother's waist. "You look beautiful."

"So do you."

"Well, I guess we know where I get my good looks from."

"Your dad?"

June laughed. "No, Mom. You." She grabbed her bouquet off the dresser, passing it to her. "Are you ready?"

Gertie nodded. She exited the bedroom and walked downstairs; June trailing behind to make sure she didn't trip on her skirt. She gulped down several deep breaths, her chest suddenly feeling shallow, her nerves prickling throughout her body. She made her way to the back door, following the trail of daisy petals that led into the backyard. June hooked her arm through hers, and then they were out the door.

As soon as she crossed the threshold, Gertie locked eyes with Bea. Undeniably handsome, standing there in her tux, her hair brushed back. She laughed when she saw the shock spread across Bea's face, those silver eyes sparkling with delight. Bea's knees buckled, her hand pressed to her heart as though trying to catch her breath. The audience chuckled, a few people clapped. Once at the altar, June kissed her cheek, and hugged her tightly. Gertie blinked away the tears that rose in her eyes as she watched her join the other bridesmaids.

Then it was just her, Bea, and their officiant. For a moment it was as though they were suspended in time, Bea marveling at the sight of her, drinking her in as though she were a fine glass of wine. She watched as tears welled in her eyes, and Bea choked back a sob.

She had waited her whole life for this.

Bea cupped her face in her hands. "Wow." She wiped away a tear of Gertie's with her thumb. "You are...my dream come true."

Gertie swallowed back a sob. "You're mine, too."

They leaned in a little too close, at which point the officiant intervened to stop them from kissing. The audience laughed up-roariously, and Kellyanne shouted something like, "They can't keep their hands off each other! See? *See?*" which only made peo-ple laugh harder. After a few minutes, everyone finally settled down, and they began the ceremony, the officiant starting some long-ass—admittedly lovely—speech about love or whatever. Gertie scanned the audience quickly, making note of the guests, the flower arrangements, the security guards Kayle had posted that lingered at the back of the yard, closest to the doors.

As the officiant continued to read, she noticed something strange. A woman in a dress, exiting through the back doors. *Hmm.* Probably a guest that had been in the bathroom? Maybe a late arrival? But when she stepped into the yard, Gertie realized with a sickening horror that wasn't the case. Lorelai, ax in hand, delivered a blow to one of the guards, who instantly crumpled.

Well, the bitch had been smart about one thing: this was the perfect moment to catch them off guard.

Twenty-Three

YOU WOULD THINK THAT in a crowd of fifty plus people, at least one person would step up to stop the deranged lunatic with an ax, but unfortunately, you'd be wrong. Once Lorelai dug out her weapon from the guard, she went after another guest, cracking open the back of his head. Bone and flesh exploded like a confetti cannon, raining down on her and the surrounding guests. Her filthy tongue swiped around the edges of her chapped lips. Screaming, people fled their seats, some running into the house, others further into the backyard, some back to their cars parked in the front. Just as one of the guards removed his pistol to fire at her, she whipped the ax at him boomerang-style, striking him in his arm, a geyser of blood gushing from the open wound. With an agonized shout, he dropped his pistol and it fired; striking another partygoer in the foot. The man shrieked as blood poured from the gash and bone and bits of leather from his shoe twisted together.

Gertie immediately flocked to the kids, pushing them in the direction of the woods. "June, River, *go*."

Her children stared back at her, stunned, eyes wide and glassy like porcelain dolls. Holland joined them from the crowd, shaking, his face an unusual shade of green. He looped his hand through River's and pulled him toward the woods. But June remained in place.

"No, Mommy," June whispered. "I'm not leaving you."

Lorelai yanked out the ax from the guard's arm and Gertie hugged June to her chest, shielding her from the horror to follow. One strike to the throat was all she needed to defeat him. June choked down a sob as she listened to the sickening squelches that followed. Geysers of blood spurted from the severed arteries, staining the rented white chairs red, sprinkling across the front lawn and soaking into the earth. The guard clutched as his throat and attempted to wriggle backward, only for her to bring the ax down again, splitting his face in half. Gertie winced, watching as his skull caved in and his nose crushed into the remains of his bloody mouth. Bloodshot eyes popped from the decimated skull, rolling onto the ground.

"Mom, please, I can't, please don't make me—"

At that moment, Winnie and Zoya rushed up, grabbing June by the arms and dragging her in the direction of the woods. Gertie watched her go, swallowing a lump in her throat. Bea's hand looped through hers, and she moved in front of her as though to protect her from their ever-encroaching enemy, who stumbled forward on unsteady feet. Lorelai crept down the center of the aisle, seething, her rotten teeth clenched together. Something foul—probably pus from an abscessed tooth—dribbled out of her mouth, yellow and liquefied. Her tangled hair reached down to her waist, and streaks of dirt covered her sickly ivory skin. When she looked at them, her eyes were completely black. Hollow. Empty. For a moment, Gertie wondered if she was possessed, but then she realized—*no*. Drugs. She was on drugs.

How had this bitch gotten drugs?

"Sorry to crash the wedding, bitches," Lorelai snarled, tightening her grip on the ax. "But if *I* can't have a happy marriage, there's no way in hell you're having one."

Gertie snorted. "If you wanted that, you could've tried *not* marrying a pedophile."

"She was asking for it," Lorelai scoffed.

For a moment, Gertie forgot she didn't have a fucking weapon. "And you're asking for me to lop your brainless head off your crooked ass spine, you two-bit skank."

Enraged, Lorelai swung at them, and Bea tugged Gertie out of the way, the two of them sprinting back into the house. Gertie heard Kayle shouting and gunshots firing, the bullets whizzing and striking the side of the house. They barreled down the front hall, the door wide open, their car with the *Just Married* stickers in sight. As they attempted to cross the threshold of the front door, Gertie tripped, the skirt of her dress caught in the door. Pain exploded in her ankle as she hit the porch steps, and cussing, she tried to tug her skirt out of the way. Lorelai cackled with delight as she staggered through the backdoor, a visible gunshot wound glimmering in her shoulder like a ruby freshly excavated from the earth.

"Bea," Gertie said, panic rising in the back of her throat, "I can't—I can't get up, I..."

Bea grimaced as she moved in front of Gertie. One hand reached into the umbrella holder by their door, and as she pulled one out, she fully extended it. Squaring her shoulders, she charged at Lorelai with the umbrella. Bewildered, Lorelai attempted to chop through the umbrella, and as she did, she struck the wall. With a snarled scream, Bea shoulder-checked her through the living room doorway. Gertie screamed for Bea, finally ripping her dress free, and wincing, scrambled to her feet and into the room. The two were tumbling across the floor, rolling around in a writhing mess. Gertie rushed over, and attempted to rip Lorelai off of Bea, only for the woman to wrench free of her grasp and pin her against the sofa.

"What the fuck?" Gertie screamed, her hands attempting to scratch and push back against the wildcat of a woman. "Are you on coke!? Who gave you coke?!"

Lorelai's grubby little hands found their way to the base of Gertie's throat, squeezing tight, and Gertie's body clenched, rasping for air. Bea scrambled toward the fireplace, grabbed one of the pokers, and with a mighty scream, thrust it through Lorelai's abdomen. The woman shrieked, her hands releasing Gertie's throat and moving to the steel tip that protruded from her stomach. Blood bubbled from the wound, dribbling onto Gertie's formerly perfect white dress. Strips of intestine twisted outward from the gash, sloshing onto the couch.

"Keep your fucking hands off my wife!"

Bea yanked the poker from her stomach, then thrust it in again, and again. Lorelai howled with pain, writhing on the ground, now pleading for mercy, but Bea didn't relent. Lorelai slunk down from the couch, holding her hands up to block the blows, but Bea kept hammering it down, whacking her over and over again. Gashes and lacerations crisscrossed their way across the woman's body; chunks of flesh splattered across the floor and coffee table. Within seconds her face became a soup of blood and bone, unrecognizable. Stunned, Gertie watched as Bea continued till Lorelai no longer made a sound. Her entrails spilled from her multiple stab wounds, and blood soaked into the carpet Wesley had died on.

Fuck, they were going to have to replace the carpet this time.

Panting, Bea hovered over the corpse, wiping the blood and sweat from her face. She threw the weapon on the floor with a disgusted snarl, then looked at Gertie, silver eyes wide.

"You okay?"

Gertie nodded, eyes welling with tears. Bea crouched in front of her, cupping her face in her hands, before embracing her tightly.

"You know we're not officially married yet, right?" Gertie sniffled. "She ruined it. We didn't sign the marriage license. You didn't get to hear my vows. You..."

In the minutes before the police arrived, they grieved for what they had lost.

Twenty-Four

A S IT TURNED OUT, shitty little Lorelai had been watching the house since the night before the wedding. They found several food wrappers and a makeshift sleeping structure in the woods nearby. Kayle had been posted outside the house to keep watch along with another guard, but when he went to take a piss, Lorelai had snuck up and taken out one of them. With all the surrounding trees and foliage that they had planted over the past year, she'd been given the perfect cover to approach the venue. The guard hadn't seen her coming.

With their home now a crime scene for four homicides and one aggravated assault, the Burns-Robinson family was forced to move into an Airbnb until an investigation could be concluded. Not only had Gertie lost the chance to have the wedding of her dreams, she also had to live with the nightmare that the cops may uncover everything that happened in that house, although Kayle had assured her it wouldn't happen.

"They're not going to find out about Earl or Westley," he said. "And even if they suspected anything, there're a couple guys on the force that are easy to buy off."

To Kayle's credit, he was right. 72 hours later, the investigation was concluded. The evidence Kayle had planted in the original murder of Ernest included some hateful rants about Bea, accusing her of robbing them of their happiness for various reasons. Using these diary entries, the police determined Lorelai targeted Bea out of jealousy. In all honesty, the whole fiasco was quite embarrassing for the police, who had failed to find Lorelai after she had "murdered" Ernest.

After hiring a crime scene clean-up crew and getting the carpet replaced, the family returned home within a week, each of them forever changed for the worse. Gertie couldn't even look at the kids without feeling immense waves of guilt over the trauma they had endured. At her core, she knew this was her fault, not Kayle's. Had she not enacted revenge against Ernest, this wouldn't have happened. She thought she had learned this lesson already, but she hadn't.

And that was eating her alive.

She couldn't eat, instead retiring to her room to sleep for hours at a time. For once, she was completely unmotivated to go to work. Bea was more supportive than ever before, helping her bathe and comb her hair, cooking her meals, and cuddling with her. Even though Bea was hurting too, she was able to set aside that grief to help her.

Gertie hadn't loved her harder.

After two weeks of wasting away, June knocked on their bedroom door and entered, her ridiculous little planner in hand. She held it up, swallowing back a lump in her throat, chin raised in determination.

"Mom. Bea. Get dressed and come downstairs. We need to talk."

"About what?" Gertie grumbled.

"Please don't argue, Mommy. Come with me."

With a heavy sigh, Gertie climbed out of bed and put on her robe. Hand in hand with Bea, they trudged downstairs and into their newly redone living room, where to their surprise, several of their friends and family members were sitting. River, Kellyanne, Zoya, Kayle, and even Holland, all on the edge of their seats. A giant whiteboard rested on an easel, with notes scribbled across it.

BEA AND GERTIE WEDDING 2.0

Gertie couldn't hide her disdain. "What in fresh hell is this?"

"Sit down," June said.

"Junebug, I'm not—"

"Sit. *Down.*" June said, snapping her fingers. Her voice was calm, but her eyes were alight with anger. "Please, Mom."

Bewildered, Gertie and Bea sat down on the couch as the others offered them sympathetic smiles. June picked up a marker and tapped the whiteboard.

"I'm going to college in a few weeks. If we don't get this done *now,* you're going to have to put off your wedding for another year. And I can't let that happen. Love *has* to win."

Gertie sighed. "You cannot creatively slogan your way out of this, June. People are dead."

"And that's horrible, but how is that your fault? That means you can't get married?"

Bea and Gertie exchanged a look, then stared back at her.

Gertie scratched her head. "Uh, kinda, yeah."

"I don't think so," June said. "Actually, none of us think so. You two never had a real wedding, and you both deserve one. So I say we get it done, come hell or high water."

"What do you mean? I don't even have a dress. Bea doesn't have a tux. There's no food, there's no venue—"

"I took the liberty of calling around this past week. The boutique has a size 20 mermaid dress they're willing to rent, and a tux for Bea. The catering company felt bad about what happened and decided to throw in a small meal for twenty-five people for free, and they've also agreed to make another cake, although it can't be three-tiered like the one you had before."

Kayle chimed in. "I also have plenty of daisies, Gertie. I grew more than enough over this past year in preparation for the wedding. Me and the boys can whip up some new floral arrangements in a jiff."

"Where would we get married?"

"So glad you asked, because I called around, and while the courthouse is out of the question on Sundays... Your middle school is available!" June squealed.

Gertie blinked, and removed her glasses to clean them. Bea tilted her head to the side.

"Sorry, June, it's just—I almost thought you suggested we'd get married at our middle school," Bea said, laughing.

"I did! The library is a *perfect* place, and Martha's got people who can work on moving the bookshelves to make room for the ceremony. With that stained glass ceiling? Ugh, the pictures will be *so* killer."

"How much does that even cost?"

Kellyanne piped up. "Nothing. I spoke with Ralph—you know, he's the principal now—and he said he owed you a favor after helping the activities center get more money, so..."

River piped up. "Holland and I are willing to do whatever we need to help set up."

"And for what it's worth," Holland said, "outdoor weddings are overrated anyways. Too hot and sweaty."

June snapped her fingers like he'd delivered the sickest lines of slam poetry. "Yas, Holland, good point! *Very* good point."

Zoya waved a hand. "And no need to worry about the cost of anything else. I'll cover it. *Inshallah*, we will make this wedding happen."

Bea and Gertie stared back at them all in shock.

Kellyanne looked at Gertie, and although exhaustion ringed the undersides of her eyes, a smile was plastered across her face. "Honey, honestly, it's whatever you two want to do. We're here to support you. And I'm... I'm so angry for you." She dabbed at her eyes with a tissue. "You've had so many good things taken from you, Gertie. You deserve a win. And fuck anyone who says otherwise."

Gertie had no idea that Kellyanne cared so deeply for their friendship—honestly, she thought Kellyanne only agreed to be in the wedding for the 'gram—but now, hearing her words, a little warmth fluttered within her chest. She took a deep breath, and looked over at Bea—

—but Bea wasn't sitting beside her.

She was down on one knee, a small black box in hand. Gertie's jaw dropped open.

"Are you seriously showing up *my* proposal?" Gertie cried out, laughing.

"Ah-ah-ah—*you* never got an engagement ring." Bea smiled. "I'm only fulfilling my end of the bargain."

"Oh my god, I can't believe you and June were in on this." She wiped her eyes. "You're the worst."

Bea cracked open the lid to the box, revealing the glittering ring beneath. "Gertrude Ingrid Burns, there is *nothing,* and I mean nothing, that will keep me from spending the rest of my life with you. Will you marry me?"

Gertie knew her answer already.

Twenty-Five

T HE NEXT DAY, KAYLE showed up in a limousine to whisk the family over to the middle school. The catering company generously donated a small breakfast for them all to enjoy, which they picked apart while trying to get ready in the bathroom stalls and the dressing room beside the theater. Given the quick turn-around time of everything, this event was more chaotic than the last. Gertie found herself getting overwhelmed at the amount of shouting and rushing around, and at a certain point, she declared that she needed a break, and slipped out into the hallway.

With a huff, she wrapped her bathrobe tighter around her body, walking past the cafeteria where people were setting up for the reception. Kayle bossed his crew around, demanding they help the DJ set up and place floral arrangements. Gertie's nervous hands moved to her mouth to chew on her fingernails, but she stopped herself—or rather, the person she bumped into stopped her.

"Shit, sorry..." Gertie looked up, eyes wide. "Bea."

Bea was wearing her shirt, but not her suit jacket. She looked a little pale, but smiled at Gertie warmly. "Nervous?"

"Nervous doesn't begin to describe how I feel right now."

"I am, too. I mean, hopefully no one is going to crash our wedding and start killing guests, but..."

"If you think about it, this is our third time getting married. Third time's the charm, isn't that how the saying goes?"

Bea laughed. "Maybe you're right."

Gertie sighed, looking around the space. It was at that moment that she realized they were standing right in front of the bathroom where they had their final altercation in middle school. Bea seemed to realize it at the same time that she did, swallowing a nervous lump in her throat.

Gertie nudged her, a playful smile on her lips. "You got a little morbid curiosity?"

"Curiosity..." She let the question hang.

Gertie squeezed her hand. "Come on."

Bea laughed as Gertie led her through the door, and it closed behind them with a soft thump. The tile here was the same sky blue it had been when they were kids, but the stalls had been upgraded; no longer the rusty red death boxes they'd been forced to squeeze into, but instead more spacious stalls in a serene white.

"Wow," Bea whispered. "It's actually like, nice in here now. It's changed a lot."

So have we, Gertie thought, watching as Bea examined the tiles surrounding the mirror. Back then, people used to scrawl on the tiles in Sharpie. *Jessica loves Brady. Vanessa is a fugly bitch. Gullible is written on the ceiling*—that one was true, a couple of girls had stood on each other's shoulders to write it up there one day, and it hadn't been erased since. The wall served as a place to curse those you hated, and a place to wish for good luck.

"Look at that." Bea motioned Gertie to come closer. "It's still there."

"What? What is it?" Gertie leaned close, and saw what was written on it.

BR & GT

Beatrice Robinson. Gertie Taylor. Right in the center of a heart outline.

"You wrote our initials back here?"

"Um... This is sort of fucked up, but yeah. I was convinced *that* day...you'd be my girlfriend. Delusional. So, *so* delusional."

Gertie smirked. "I wasn't your girlfriend, but at least I'm going to be your wife."

"Right? So maybe this bathroom is lucky after all."

"Mmm..." Gertie leaned against her. "Or maybe you're just hot."

Bea giggled. Gertie ran her fingers through her hair. Standing this close to her, she smelled so tantalizing. Cedar invaded her nostrils as she pressed her lips against Bea's neck. Bea chuckled as her hands moved to her waist.

"You're going to smudge your lipstick."

"That makeup artist is paid by the hour," Gertie replied, nuzzling her neck. "She'll earn her money's worth." She stopped, glanced over her shoulder, then looked back at their reflection. "Humor me for a sec?"

Bashful, Bea nodded, following her inside one of the stalls. Gertie locked the door behind them, pressing her up against it, kissing her lips. Some strange sensation had overcome her, far more intoxicating than liquor, but she quite liked it.

"Have you ever wondered what would've happened that day if I hadn't rejected you?"

Bea's eyebrows rose. "You mean... Oh wow." Bea tilted her head up to the ceiling, blushing red. She buried her face in her hands, but Gertie peeled them away, kissing her palms and squeezing them.

"I don't want this place to hold so much negative energy over us," Gertie whispered. "So...last night I was thinking... What if we rewrote our history? You always wondered what it would be like if things had been different. This is a chance to explore that."

"Wait a minute, you're suggesting we *role play* the incident that mutually traumatized us?"

"Y-yeah. I mean, remember when we used the lipstick? We had fun then, didn't we?"

A blush filled Bea's cheeks. "Oh yeah."

"And why was it fun?"

"Because... Well, it took away a lot of shame I had. And I was fulfilling a longtime fantasy."

"I mean, in a way, wasn't what happened back then, um, a fantasy too?"

Bea considered this. "I mean... Yeah. Yeah, I guess it was. I wanted to—yeah." She sighed. "So you're serious about this, huh?"

Gertie nodded. "No shame, no judgment, no fear. You can walk out the door if you want and finish getting ready, or we can give this a shot. I won't judge you either way."

Bea blinked, staring at her. "This is kinda crazy."

"No crazier than eating a used tampon, Bea."

"Are we talking the same rules?"

"Yes, of course. Just don't slam me into the tiles or anything, that'd hurt like a bitch."

Bea took a deep breath, exhaled, and placed her hands on her hips. "Okay. Well, if that's the case, then...then I would've told you that day you looked pretty." Bea smiled, cheeks red and bashful as she took her hands. "You were wearing this gingham skirt and oversized sweater. Couldn't stop staring at your butt."

Gertie laughed. "You remember my outfit?"

"I remember all of it." Bea's fingers twirled through her curls. Gertie smiled at her tenderness, closing her eyes. Back then Bea had touched her face like this, and at the time, she'd been disgusted, but now she was filled with nothing but warmth. "I remember you answering all those questions in Ms. Hanson's class about *Watership Down* and the way your nose crinkled with satisfaction when you answered every question right. I remember thinking I'd want to make you smile like that."

Gertie leaned forward as though to kiss her but resisted. Her cheeks burned, desperate to be touched. She had to wait for Bea to tell her what was next. She waited with bated breath as Bea unwrapped her robe, and she flinched as the cold air touched her bare skin. Bea's hands trailed over her hips, her fingers playing with the waistband of her panties.

"Gertie," Bea whispered, "can you show it to me?"

"Sure." Gertie shivered as Bea slipped them off of her, and they dropped to her ankles in an underwhelming way. For a moment they stared at each other, breathless, then sputtered with laughter.

"This is so gross."

Bea's eyes examined her, the smile still on her face. "I don't know what I was thinking. At this angle I can't see much of anything."

"I don't think *seeing* was your entire goal back then."

"No, it wasn't." Bea bit her lip, cheeks red. Her eyes took her in once again. "Can I touch you?"

"Why do you want to touch me?" she asked, her voice gentle.

"Because I want to make you feel the best you've ever felt in your life. Would you let me?"

Gertie's mouth ran dry. Her *yes* left her mouth in a whisper. Bea inserted her finger into her mouth, sucking on it, and then tentatively used it to explore her clit. It felt experimental and awkward, but Gertie shivered, biting her lip as her finger circled around and around. A shuddery breath escaped Bea's lips, and Gertie noticed that look in her eyes, familiar. It was the same look she had when she put on the strapless dress.

"Hey, Bea?"

"Yeah?"

"Is this the part when you would've kissed me?"

"Fuck yeah."

The rest of the wedding went off without a hitch. June gave Gertie to Bea as she had before, and the officiant delivered their speech, albeit a little bit faster than she had at their first wedding. Then it came time for them to read their vows. Gertie spoke about Bea's strengths and her tenderness. Bea sniffled, wiping away the tears in her eyes. When it was her turn to speak, she took Gertie's hands in hers.

"I had things written down on notecards, but I don't need them," Bea whispered. "Because everything I love about you has been ingrained in me since we were old enough to write our names. Your beauty, your intelligence, your confidence—just—god, I've never run out of reasons to fall deeper in love with you, and I know I never will.

"When I first met you, all those years ago...you awakened a fire in me like nothing else. That first day of school, I'd forgotten my lunch at home. I had no money, couldn't call my parents for help, since they'd—well, that's not appropriate for this venue, but...Gertie, you stepped up to help me. You were the one who shared your snack with me when I came in crying after recess because I didn't have anything to eat. You were the only one who noticed me, and you were sitting on the other side of the room."

Gertie's eyes widened as the memory came back to her. She remembered how Bea had smiled as she crunched into one of her

Ritz bits, her cherub cheeks rosy, her eyes glossy with gratitude as she murmured a thank you. It was such a small act of kindness that she hadn't thought anything of it, but Bea had never forgotten it.

"I know on the surface that you're tenacious, tough, and unshakable, but Gertie, my favorite thing about you is how compassionate you are. You have such strong convictions to help others, even when you get nothing in return. Sometimes people have scorned you, or haven't treated you as you should have been treated.

"When we met at that restaurant, I had nothing to offer you, other than my company. You had no reason to open your heart to me, and you did, over and over again, even when I wasn't at my best. To spend the rest of my life in devotion to you is a blessing I never believed I'd be graced with. I will never underestimate you, I will never hold you back, and I will never back down from anything you want to do. Your dreams are my dreams, and when I'm with you, I'm the best version of myself."

Her eyes welled with tears. The officiant held her breath as she glanced between them.

"Do you, Gertrude Burns, take Beatrice Robinson as your wife, in holy matrimony, for as long as you both shall live?"

For the second time that day, Gertie's *yes* left her mouth in a whisper.

Twenty-Six

SURPRISINGLY, A SCHOOL CAFETERIA was not a bad place for a wedding reception. Supply guests with booze, add some flashing lights, and throw in one mediocre DJ, and you had a recipe for a good time. The guests boogied and laughed, their voices drowned out by the sounds of the music. Gertie and Bea had their first dance to a Hozier song, and each of the kids danced with their mothers.

Breathless, Gertie took a break while Bea encouraged all the guests to dance the Macarena. She joined Zoya, who was also taking a break, fanning herself with a fistful of napkins.

"Hello, gorgeous," Zoya said, patting the seat beside her.

Gertie laughed as she plopped down. "Am I that really that pretty when my sweat's smeared all my makeup?"

"You were so gorgeous your wife couldn't help herself well before you got to the altar today, m'dear. Yes." Zoya chuckled. "How's it feel? Being married again?"

"Like a dream. Here's hoping I don't wake up."

Zoya held up her glass of water. "Cheers to that."

They clinked glasses, each taking a sip. Gertie watched as Bea danced with their guests, making them laugh. Zoya smiled.

"You're so in love."

"I really am. It's kinda dorky."

"No, not at all. After everything you've been through, you deserve to be hopelessly in love. Trust in that."

"Thank you. And...thank you for doing all of this for me," Gertie whispered. "I don't know how I could ever repay you."

Zoya arched a brow, confused. "Who said anything about you repaying me?"

"You're sure you don't need anything from me, or there's nothing I can do for you?"

"Gertie." Zoya smoothed out her skirt. "I know in our world, everything can be misconstrued as a favor, but believe me, I want nothing more than for you to have a good wedding. That's why we all pitched in."

"Sorry," Gertie mumbled, feeling bashful. She tucked a strand of sweaty hair behind her ear. "I guess—it's like what Bea said in her vows. Been burned a bit. Honestly, I'm surprised that Kellyanne showed up for me. I didn't think we were that close."

Zoya smirked. "I figured, given the incident with Misty."

Slowly, Gertie turned to look at her.

"You're not the only one who uses a private investigator. Or Google, for that matter."

"O-oh. Shit." Gertie coughed a little, cheeks burning with embarrassment.

"You and I, Gertie, we're friends because we're alike. We're sharks in open water. Together, we can take down giants. Whales, if you will."

Gertie stared at her. "What are you talking about?"

Zoya laughed, elbowing her. A Cheshire cat smile spread across her lips. "I hope you don't mind, but after this whole incident with that psychopath... I had to do a little digging. There were some things about how this all unfolded... I mean, they weren't adding up. I don't even know who would've let Ernest out in the first place..."

She reached into her purse, and withdrew a stack of Polaroids.

"What are these?" Gertie whispered, her voice dropping low.

"It's the last wedding present I have for you. I wanted to wait until later, but you're going to want to hit up that honeymoon suite, so..."

With wide eyes, Gertie flipped through them. Her mouth dropped open in shock. She looked up at Zoya, who simply nodded in response.

"You're—you're kidding me. *She's* why he got released from prison? *She* started all of this?" Gertie seethed with anger. "I'll kill her."

"No need for bloodshed, my dear. And no crying, either, you'll ruin your makeup," Zoya replied. "I know *exactly* what we have to do."

"We?" Gertie asked.

"Yes. You, me, Winnie, Norah, Laura... All of us." Zoya patted her hand. "Go dance with your wife, beloved. I will take care of everything else."

What Gertie found in those photos was cold, hard, incriminating evidence. The judge that had presided over Ernest's parole decision, Thomas Buren, exiting Heather Harrelson's office. Buren walking alongside Harrelson with Starbucks cups in hand. Buren exiting Harrelson's car at night.

Heather.

Heather Harrelson had been the reason why Ernest got out on parole.

Now, Zoya didn't know the answer as to why, so Gertie went back to Kayle, who did yet another deep dive, and what he dug up was quite shocking. While her old bitter-bitch rival Misty Brightly didn't have any siblings, she did have a cousin she was close to: Marie *Heather* Adkisson, who grew up to be Heather Harrelson. Years of plastic surgery in her early 20s made Heather virtually unrecognizable to her younger self.

This bitter, vindictive bitch had advocated for Ernest's release from prison for the sole purpose of getting back at Gertie.

"This absolute fucking cunt!" Gertie raved, whipping her drink glass at the wall. It shattered into hundreds of pieces. The way that Heather had looked at her when they met. The way she had treated her, like the scum at the bottom of her shoe. Gertie thought it was weird that someone she never met would treat her with such disgust, and as it turned out, she was right.

Kayle admired the mess from where he sat at her desk. "Justified."

"What the fuck? Misty's not even dead. She lost her fucking mind, not that she had much of one to begin with."

"What's Zoya's plan?" Bea asked.

Gertie called up her friend on speakerphone to explain what she had found out. Zoya expressed shock and disgust, but assured Gertie that again, she had a plan, involving a certain clock app, and all her adoring fans. Zoya summoned her lawyers, and in the following days, Gertie met with all of her political allies to construct how they would break the news that a state senator advocated for the release of a violent pedophile. This final, delicious act of revenge would have to be the most carefully constructed plan Gertie and Bea had ever carried out—

—and thankfully, they weren't doing it alone.

Two weeks after her wedding, Gertie recorded a TikTok LIVE, unveiling everything she had learned about Heather, her connection to Misty, and how Heather had treated her so unkindly.

"My entire family's life was upended because of Heather's actions. My poor wife, who has worked so hard to overcome her trauma, suddenly had that thrust into the public eye, like it was schoolgirl gossip. Is that who you really want to represent you, Sherburne County? You want someone who is this callous and cruel to survivors of child sexual abuse?" Gertie swallowed back a lump in her throat as a single tear squeezed from the corner of her eye. "This is not someone who cares for her community. This is a ruthless monster devoid of any compassion."

Bea was waiting off camera for her queue. When Gertie looked at her, Bea came over, wrapping her in an embrace. Gertie was supposed to be acting, the tears not supposed to be genuine, but they were. She sobbed into Bea's shoulder while she held her close. Comments expressing support and countless little red hearts flooded the screen. Bea wiped away Gertie's tears, trying to address their audience.

"My wife has been nothing less than a saint," Bea said, her voice hoarse. "What happened between her and Heather's cousin has nothing to do with the fact that my uncle was a dangerous predator who should never have been released into society. Had Heather not intervened, he would still be in prison, and we would've had our original wedding without any bloodshed or violence. Lives were lost as a result of her actions. And she almost—she almost drove me to the point where I wanted to take mine."

A lie or not, this time, Gertie couldn't tell. But the audience would eat it up, and eat it up they did. Social media exploded, and when Winnie, Laura, Norah, and Zoya added their own videos, speaking about their own experiences regarding Heather being a conniving, passive aggressive bitch, well, the ambush of anger that descended on their little suburban communities was near-ly enough to start a riot. People lined up outside of Heather's office, and on television, Gertie and Bea delighted in seeing the woman pelted with tomatoes and rotten vegetables. Numerous local women's organizations publicly uninvited Heather from their galas, and one returned her donation out of solidarity for Bea. The state senate, frustrated and overrun by the chaos and death threats, quickly moved to expel Heather. She became the fourth elected official expelled from the state's legislature; the very first woman to do so.

A girlboss to the very end.

Although Zoya and Gertie thought of themselves as sharks, the public was more bloodthirsty. They didn't stop at her expulsion. She became a complete social pariah, ridiculed in public places. Locals took to harassing her for views on social media. At a certain point, the police, eager to pin the blame on someone, launched an investigation into Heather, and as it turns out, she'd been funneling money and resources to Lorelai through package drops, hence why she was able to survive on nothing, and also, indulge in an expensive cocaine habit. By the time that was made public, her own kids were talking shit about her, and her husband served her divorce papers. Within three weeks, she went dark on all her platforms, becoming yet another unfortunate person who fucked around with Gertie, and found out.

Twenty-Seven

"I PROMISE, I *PROMISE*, we're going to actually plan a trip—"

"Gertie—"

"—we should go to Rome. No. Amsterdam. Everyone goes to Rome. We need to be artsy. Daring. Edgy. Amsterdam is edgy, right?"

Bea fumbled with the keys of the lake house, jamming in the lock and twisting the front door open. "We have *plenty* of time to think about it. I'm not pressed about our staycamoon."

"Staycamoon?"

"Staycation honeymoon. I mean, technically it's not a staycation honeymoon, we're in our lake house. That's a vacation, right?"

Gertie sighed as she lifted the bags over the threshold. Although they had visited this house a few times since burying Earl here, it had been a while since they last dropped by. Bea took the bags from her grasp, kissing her cheek.

"No lifting a finger," she told her. "You'll have plenty of opportunities to spoil me rotten."

Gertie chuckled and watched as Bea took the bags upstairs. She checked her phone—Kayle was watching the kids this weekend, and had made a space for himself in the guest bedroom. He sent her a picture of the kitchen, already in chaos, River and Holland covered in flour and June hurling something at them both...a bag of chocolate chips? She texted him back, telling him he had the full authority to ground them if needed.

Migrating to the kitchen, Gertie grabbed the bottle of champagne Jack's parents had gifted to them, and found a corkscrew. By the time Bea came back downstairs, two fresh glasses had been poured. They toasted, throwing back their drinks with laughter. Bea shuddered in disgust, tongue sticking out as she set the glass back down. Gertie gagged a little bit.

"What the hell is in this stuff?"

Gertie wiped at her eyes, still laughing. "This is supposed to be a nice brand."

"I tasted bubbles more than I did booze." She rifled through the fridge, pulling out a carton of orange juice that had likely seen better days, but the situation was desperate. They poured fresh glasses, mixing it with the juice, taking smaller sips this time.

"Beatrice Burns, I think you've fixed it."

"Burns..." Beatrice smiled, raising her glass for another toast. "Here's to the Burns family—for many reasons, but for being kind enough to make me a part of it, despite never having met me."

"Here's to the Burnses."

"And," Bea said, "to Jack."

Gertie smiled back. "To Jack."

It didn't take long before the two wound up in their bedroom, enveloped in each other's arms as they had been countless times before—and, the universe willing, would do far more times. Gertie pressed Bea against the mattress, kissing her neck, hand sliding underneath her shirt to caress her breast. Bea's kisses were earnest, but somehow, different; more forceful. As she pulled off her clothes, she was a bit ferocious in her movements, her hands working with an eager aggression that excited her. Nonetheless, Gertie was surprised when Bea rolled over, straddling her waist.

"Ahh, I see," Gertie said with a smirk, placing her hands on her hips. "You want to ride cowgirl style. Excellent choice, Mrs. Burns; I like a nice view."

Bea laughed, voice low and sultry. She leaned over Gertie, placing her hands on either side of her shoulders, hips grazing low against hers. "Not exactly what I was thinking..."

"Oh?" Gertie shuddered as Bea kissed her ear—her weak spot—as her wife's hand slid below the waistband of her shorts. "You want to..."

Over the past year, they'd been trying to accustom Bea to topping, primarily using dildos and vibrators, and only occasionally using the strap-on. It had been rather tame compared to what they were used to doing, but it was still fun. Over the past year, Bea had built up her confidence, something Gertie delighted in seeing. That possessive look in her eyes grew ever stronger, captivating her.

She hoped it would never let her go.

"Uh huh." Bea chuckled as she kissed her neck again. "And I might be getting ahead of myself, but I wanted to try a little something."

"What is it?"

Bea reached into the nightstand, and pulled out a belt. She snapped it, flexing the leather between her hands. Gertie swallowed a lump of nervousness in her throat as something stirred in the pit of her stomach.

"Yeah. We can try it."

Bea tied her wrists together with the belt and had Gertie lift her arms above her head. She fluffed pillows behind her, making sure she was comfortable. She sat back on the bed, appraising her handiwork, and smiled.

"Oh yeah. This is doing something for me."

"Is it?"

"Hell yeah."

Gertie laid on the bed shivering, watching as Bea removed the rest of her clothes and pulled on the strap-on. Bea took her time, teasing her with it, and she couldn't help but shiver at the sight. After applying the lube, she eagerly guided Bea inside of her, gulping down a moan.

"Feel okay?"

Gertie nodded. "Yeah."

Bea's hips rolled forward and receded back, moving slowly, trying to help her get adjusted. Gertie moaned, watching as Bea slid in and out of her. She had a burning desire to touch herself, to touch Bea, to touch *something*, but with her hands tied, it was tortuous.

Well, if she had to endure any kind of torture, she'd prefer it to be this.

KAYLE

I see her on the security camera now.

One of my guys is posted right around the corner if you need anything.

Gertie showed the text to Bea, who chuckled, shaking her head. Something solid, such as a rock, smashed through glass downstairs, and footsteps echoed afterwards. Bea shrugged her shoulders. She pushed Gertie down against the mattress, and the woman gasped as Bea wrenched apart her legs and pushed her way deep inside. She shuddered, throwing back her head, mouth open, watching as Bea thrust in and out of her pussy—like she owned it; like it was hers.

Because it was.

"I know you love an audience," Bea said with a grin. "So let's show her what a good girl you are, huh?"

"Ahh—yes... Keep going, baby. Don't stop."

The footsteps were closer now, but neither paid any attention to Heather when she entered their doorway.

"Hello, newlyweds." Heather said, her voice gravelly and yet wet, as though she had been drinking and crying. Judging from the redness of her nose and streaks of mascara rolling down her cheeks, that's exactly what she had been doing.

But they didn't look up. Bea continued to pound her, and Gertie writhed beneath, her back arching as she moaned and begged for more. Heather stood there, confused, as if unsure whether they had noticed her or not. But when Bea winked at her, she knew she had.

"Ohh—fuck!" Gertie cried out as Bea thrust in deeper. She looked over at Heather, a smirk on her face. "You know, for a homophobic bitch, you've been watching us a while. Almost like you want to join in or something."

Bea continued to move her hips, a wry smirk across her lips. "I don't share."

"No—*mmm*—I don't either." Gertie giggled. "Sorry, she's all mine."

By this point Heather seemed more distraught with the fact that the people she showed up to terrorize were continuing to fuck right in front of her. Gertie licked her hand and rubbed it between her legs.

"Keep looking at me like that," she said, shuddering. "It's so pathetic."

"What the—stop!"

"Stop?" Gertie shook her head, laughing. "That's not how this works, bitch. You wanted to crash our honeymoon, you'll get a show, too."

"You—you're both fucking disgusting," she shrieked. She reached into her pocket and withdrew a knife, pointing it at them. But neither reacted with fear.

"We're into that, too," Gertie said.

"The fuck do you mean you're into that too? *Stop!*"

"You're so shrill." Gertie huffed, looking up at Bea. "I'm losing my buzz. Can you..."

"Yep." Bea pulled out, and Gertie shuddered, but made no effort to move. While Heather stood there in confusion, Bea reached over and grabbed a gun from within the nightstand. Heather's vocal cords reacted before her feet did. The bullet struck her square in the heart, and she crumpled to the ground, gasping for air. Blood splattered over the walls and carpet, the viscous ooze dripping down like wet paint. The woman's body slumped against the door, jaw slack, eyes wide with shock.

Bea blew across the top of the pistol like a cowboy in an old school Western. "Bullseye."

"Is she still alive?"

"Not for much longer." Bea clicked the safety back on and put the weapon back in the drawer, leaving it open. "Clean shot. Probably a few more minutes at best."

"Perfect."

Gertie rolled onto her knees, staring at Heather from across the room. The woman was deflating like a balloon three days after a party. Blood evacuated the hole in her chest and spilled onto the floor, and her hands pawed at the wound in a feeble attempt to seal it. The liquid coursed up her throat, bubbling from her mouth, and as she bled, she began to choke.

Gertie moaned as Bea entered her body again, her hands digging into the sheets. "I want the last thing she sees to be you making me come. T-then we can call the cops. Remember: she broke in, you shot her, and—*uhnn*—we called as soon as we could."

"God, you're such a psycho," Bea groaned. "I'm so fucking turned on right now."

"And I," Gertie said, eyelids fluttering as Bea hit those sweet spots inside of her, "am so fucking close."

The End

Acknowledgments

In all my years of writing, I don't think I've ever created a couple of characters I loved more than Gertie and Bea. Shortly after its predecessor Vicarious released, I started to write this very sequel. Gertie and Bea are a dynamic, problematic duo that are near and dear to my heart, so getting the opportunity to revisit their story again was such a privilege.

Thank you to David-Jack and Lee for letting me write a sexier, bloodier sequel; y'all are both so rad, and I'm so happy to be back with Slashic. Also thank you to Ruth Anna Evans for her work on theVicious cover.

Thank you to every reader who has messaged me, written a review, or told me how much they loved Vicarious. I was pleasantly surprised that so many people enjoyed this tender love story at the heart of such a brutal and gruesome novella. I hope that you get as much enjoyment reading this sequel as I did writing it.

A final thank you to the many organizations that support survivors of domestic violence and sexual assault. If you are experiencing sexual or domestic violence, please know that help is available. RAINN is an organization I've contacted in the past when I needed help, and they can help you too. You can call them at 800.656.4673 or visit their website at rainn.org.

About the Author

Minnesota native Chloe Spencer(she/her) is an award-winning writer, indie gamedev, and filmmaker. She is the author of multiple sapphic horror novellas, novels, and short stories. In her spare time she enjoys playing video games, trying her best at Pilates, and cuddling with her cats. She holds a BA in Journalism from the University of Oregon and an MFA in Film and Television from SCAD Atlanta.